013

REKI KAWAHARA ABEC bee-pee

SWORD ART ONLINE
Alicization dividing

SWORD ART ONLINE

"I don't recognize that stance, boy. Do you use the continuous blade?"

Bercouli Synthesis One § The most powerful Integrity Knight and wielder of the Time-Splitting Sword.

"...You sound very confident."

Eugeo § The first resident of this world whom Kirito met. He has joined Kirito in seeking out the top floor of Central Cathedral on a quest to rescue his childhood friend, Alice.

"Alice Zuberg...
That's...my...name?
...I can't remember any of it..."

Alice Synthesis Thirty § The girl Eugeo has been seeking. An Integrity Knight and wielder of the Osmanthus Blade.

"Your real name is Alice Zuberg...
The you right now is a false Alice
created by Administrator."

Kirito § A boy who found himself within the mysterious fantasy realm
known as the Underworld. He is striving toward the top floor
of Central Cathedral for the means to escape back to reality.

"I have nothing more to say to you.
Let's fight...That's why you're here, isn't it?"

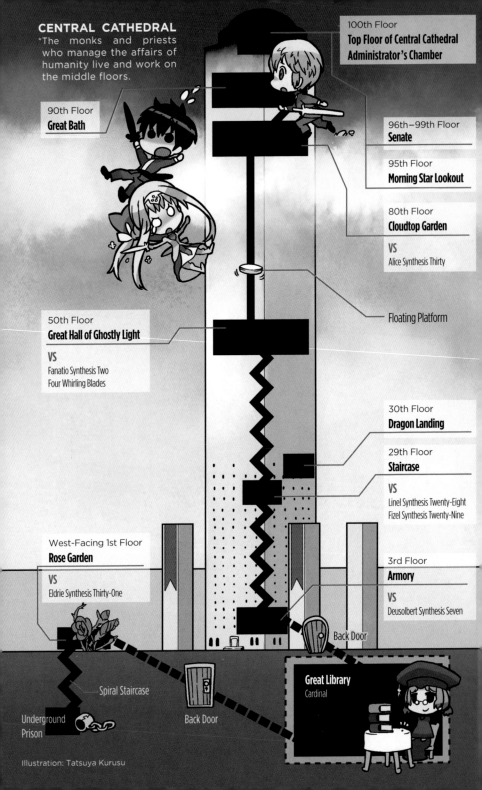

CENTRAL CATHEDRAL

*The monks and priests who manage the affairs of humanity live and work on the middle floors.

100th Floor
Top Floor of Central Cathedral
Administrator's Chamber

90th Floor
Great Bath

96th–99th Floor
Senate

95th Floor
Morning Star Lookout

80th Floor
Cloudtop Garden

VS
Alice Synthesis Thirty

Floating Platform

50th Floor
Great Hall of Ghostly Light

VS
Fanatio Synthesis Two
Four Whirling Blades

30th Floor
Dragon Landing

29th Floor
Staircase

VS
Linel Synthesis Twenty-Eight
Fizel Synthesis Twenty-Nine

West-Facing 1st Floor
Rose Garden

VS
Eldrie Synthesis Thirty-One

3rd Floor
Armory

VS
Deusolbert Synthesis Seven

Back Door

Spiral Staircase

Great Library
Cardinal

Underground
Prison

Back Door

Illustration: Tatsuya Kurusu

SWORD ART ONLINE
Alicization dividing

VOLUME 13

Reki Kawahara

abec

bee-pee

YEN ON

NEW YORK

SWORD ART ONLINE, Volume 13: ALICIZATION DIVIDING
REKI KAWAHARA

Translation by Stephen Paul
Cover art by abec

SWORD ART ONLINE Vol.13
©REKI KAWAHARA 2013
Edited by ASCII MEDIA WORKS
First published in Japan in 2013 by KADOKAWA CORPORATION, Tokyo.
English translation rights arranged with KADOKAWA CORPORATION, Tokyo,
through Tuttle-Mori Agency, Inc., Tokyo.

English translation © 2018 by Yen Press, LLC

Yen On
1290 Avenue of the Americas
New York, NY 10104

Visit us at yenpress.com
facebook.com/yenpress
twitter.com/yenpress
yenpress.tumblr.com
instagram.com/yenpress

First Yen On Edition: April 2018

Yen On is an imprint of Yen Press, LLC.
The Yen On name and logo are trademarks of Yen Press, LLC.

Library of Congress Cataloging-in-Publication Data
Names: Kawahara, Reki, author. | Abec, 1985– illustrator. | Paul, Stephen, translator.
Title: Sword art online / Reki Kawahara, abec ; translation, Stephen Paul.
Description: First Yen On edition. | New York, NY : Yen On, 2014–
Identifiers: LCCN 2014001175 | ISBN 9780316371247 (v. 1 : pbk.) |
    ISBN 9780316376815 (v. 2 : pbk.) | ISBN 9780316296427 (v. 3 : pbk.) |
    ISBN 9780316296434 (v. 4 : pbk.) | ISBN 9780316296441 (v. 5 : pbk.) |
    ISBN 9780316296458 (v. 6 : pbk.) | ISBN 9780316390408 (v. 7 : pbk.) |
    ISBN 9780316390415 (v. 8 : pbk.) | ISBN 9780316390422 (v. 9 : pbk.) |
    ISBN 9780316390439 (v. 10 : pbk.) | ISBN 9780316390446 (v. 11 : pbk.) |
    ISBN 9780316390453 (v. 12 : pbk.) | ISBN 9780316390460 (v. 13 : pbk.)
Subjects: | CYAC: Science fiction. | BISAC: FICTION / Science Fiction / Adventure.
Classification: pz7.K1755Ain 2014 | DDC [Fic]—dc23
LC record available at https://lccn.loc.gov/2014001175

ISBNs: 978-0-316-39046-0 (paperback)
        978-0-316-56105-1 (ebook)

10 9 8 7 6 5 4 3 2 1

LSC-C

Printed in the United States of America

"THIS MIGHT BE A GAME, BUT IT'S NOT SOMETHING YOU PLAY."

—Akihiko Kayaba, *Sword Art Online* programmer

SWORD ART ONLINE
Alicization dividing

Reki Kawahara

abec

bee-pee

INTERLUDE IV

JULY 6TH, 2026

The floating science facility *Ocean Turtle*, a mammoth structure nearly a quarter mile long and over an eighth of a mile wide, consisted of twelve decks, also known as levels.

By comparison, the world's largest cruise ship, *Oasis of the Seas*, was smaller and had eighteen decks—so there was an air of even greater luxury on the *Ocean Turtle*. However, given that its purpose was not leisure but oceanic scientific research, it made sense that the various observational and analytical devices would need extra room. Asuna certainly wasn't going to complain about having more space overhead.

The first deck under the waterline was the float deck; the second, just above it, was the mechanical deck; and decks three through eight were dedicated to various types of research: marine biology, deep-sea resources, plate structure, and so on. The ninth and tenth decks were for cabins; the eleventh was for recreation: sporting lounges, gyms, and a pool; and the twelfth and top deck contained radars, antennas, and observation points.

Officially, the *Ocean Turtle* belonged to JAMSTEC, the Japan Agency for Marine-Earth Science and Technology, but that was only half the truth. As the craft was propelled by a domestically produced nuclear power reactor, it had to be constructed with the help of the Self-Defense Force, and it continued to be manned by SDF soldiers at all times for security now that it was operational.

Beyond that, the composite titanium-alloy pillar that ran through the center of the ship—the Main Shaft—was completely under SDF jurisdiction, where they conducted top-secret research that had nothing to do with marine science. They were replicating newborn souls and growing them within a virtual environment in an attempt to build the world's first true bottom-up artificial intelligence: Project Alicization.

7:45 AM, Monday, July 6th, 2026.

After paying a visit to Kazuto Kirigaya (Kirito) in the medical area of the Upper Shaft, where he was still recuperating, Asuna Yuuki took breakfast in the eleventh-deck lounge with Dr. Rinko Koujiro, an expert researcher on full-dive technology.

It wasn't a luxury cruise liner, but the buffet-style food was actually pretty good—not that Asuna was going to complain about that or her cabin, given that Lieutenant Colonel Seijirou Kikuoka could snap his fingers and have her sent to the brig, if the facility indeed had such a thing.

Across from her, Rinko stuck her knife through a white fish fritter and held it up to examine the meat. "Do you suppose they caught this fish here?"

"I…I don't know…," Asuna said, looking at the same thing on her plate. She brought a piece up to her mouth. The pale fish was soft and crumbly, yet had a juicy texture. It was obviously very fresh, but she didn't know whether you could simply toss a reel out in the open ocean like this and catch something.

Asuna put down her knife and picked up her glass of iced tea as she turned her gaze to the window on her left. The calm ocean surface was dark and flat, revealing no fishing craft, much less any actual fish.

Thinking about it, all she knew was that the *Ocean Turtle* was located somewhere in the Izu Islands, which were widely spaced across a large expanse of ocean, north to south. Hachijojima was in the center of the archipelago, and that island itself was nearly two hundred miles from Tokyo.

If she could freely use her phone, she could have just pulled up a map program to pinpoint their location, but for various security reasons, she wasn't allowed to connect to the megafloat's Wi-Fi. She could still listen to her saved music files, which was better than having the phone confiscated entirely, but there was definitely something frustrating about having a smartphone and being unable to use it to instantly look up information. She hadn't even been this frustrated during *SAO*, when she had neither Internet-searching capabilities nor any news from the real world whatsoever.

Asuna swallowed the lump of annoyance along with her iced tea and tried to change her mood. Being this angry about lacking Internet access was simply a reflection of her overall deficit of necessary information.

Was what Seijirou Kikuoka and Takeru Higa told her about their project yesterday the whole truth? Were there more secrets about their test universe, the Underworld, that they hadn't explained yet? And was Nurse Natsuki Aki being honest when she claimed that Kazuto would wake up from Soul Translator Unit Four tomorrow...?

The first two were one thing, but she had to cast aside her doubts about the third. Now was the time for her to have faith. On July 7th, Kazuto's damaged neural network would finish its repair, and he would awaken. Asuna had to leave on a helicopter for Tokyo that evening, but she would at least have time to speak with him. She'd have time to hold the body that had sacrificed itself to protect her.

The thought of this moment brought some strength to her mind. She resumed eating and asked Rinko, "Do you know where exactly this ship is located? All I heard was that it's in the Izu Islands."

"...You know, that might be the extent of my knowledge, too..."

Rinko had already finished her fish. She put her hand into her coat pocket to take out her phone, then remembered she wouldn't be able to connect to the Internet anyway and scowled.

"Well, I'm pretty sure that Higa said we were a hundred miles or so west of Mikurajima…or was it Miyakejima?" she wondered, then turned her eyes to the window, which was large for a ship. Asuna followed her lead and looked out at the blue-black surface of the water again.

The morning sun was coming up through the windows behind them, meaning that they were looking to the west now. If it was true that the *Ocean Turtle* was on the western side of the Izu Islands, they wouldn't see *either* Mikurajima or Miyakejima, and certainly not the Japanese mainland of Honshu…

As her gaze swept from right to left, Asuna couldn't help but gasp. There was something out there she hadn't seen the last time, shining in the morning sun. Something artificial and narrow in the distant sea—a ship. It was hard to grasp its scale without knowing how close it was, but it seemed very large.

"Rinko, look there," she said, putting down the knife and pointing.

The other woman squinted and muttered, "That's a ship. It's… probably not the fishing boat that caught our breakfast…"

"It's not? How can you tell?"

"It's too big for that and too plainly colored. Plus…it's got a whole load of antennas on it."

Rinko got up and walked over to the window, so Asuna joined her. Asuna's eyesight was perfectly fine, but the water vapor coming off the surface made the distant ship vague and wavering. And she was right that the mast in the center of the boat seemed to be sporting a number of round satellite dishes. It resembled the massive antenna mast that rose from the top deck not far above this lounge. The design of the ship seemed pointed, angular. Not like a fishing boat but like a transport ship or…

"A warship…?" Asuna murmured.

Behind her, an officious voice stated, "That is a Japanese ship. The country does not possess any battleships."

The two women turned around and saw a man in a pure-white short-sleeved uniform, carrying his breakfast tray—Lieutenant Nakanishi.

"Good morning, Mr. Nakanishi."

"Good morning."

The tall man set down his tray on a nearby table and crisply gave them a bowed salute. "Good morning, Dr. Koujiro, Miss Yuuki."

"Would you like to sit with us?" Rinko offered. He appeared to think it over, then accepted. Asuna and Rinko waited for him to bring his tray over before they sat down again. The officer's breakfast was a hearty military one, the plate piled high with eggs, bacon, and salad.

"How does it compare to the breakfast in the SDF?" Rinko asked, a rather sensitive question.

Nakanishi grimaced and lifted his fork. "To be honest, it's slightly better here. The tomatoes and cucumbers are grown on the ship, for example."

"Whoa, there's a garden here?" Asuna exclaimed.

The officer beamed with pride. "That's right, on the rear eighth deck. It's an experiment in large-scale marine farming."

"So that's why the tomatoes tasted a bit salty," Rinko joked.

"Really?" he said, popping the slice into his mouth. Asuna couldn't help but giggle. She picked up her fork and knife to continue eating, then recalled the first thing Nakanishi had mentioned.

He had said that Japan had no battleships, but that couldn't be true. He was an SDF naval officer, so he worked on a battleship... right? Or was the logic that the SDF wasn't a proper military, which meant that their ships weren't "battle" ships? So the ship out there must have been...

Asuna looked out the window again, staring at the large, angled silhouette. "Then if it's not a warship, it's...a self-defense ship?"

"Close. SDF naval vessels are called escort ships," Nakanishi replied with a grin. He turned his head to look at it, too. "That ship is our latest general-purpose craft, the DD-127 *Nagato*. Unfortunately, I can't reveal the reason why it's traveling this stretch of…hmm?"

His concise explanation trailed off, drawing her interest back to the ship. The gray battle—er, escort—ship was beginning to change direction. In less than ten seconds, it turned so its stern was facing the *Ocean Turtle*, and it began to chug away.

Nakanishi abruptly stood up and turned away from the women so he could remove a thin device from his pocket. He pressed a few buttons and brought it to his ear to murmur, "This is Nakanishi. I'm sorry to bother you on your break, Lieutenant Colonel Kikuoka. I believe the *Nagato* was scheduled to accompany us until twelve hundred hours two days hence, but it just turned to move westward…Yes, sir, I'll be right there."

He turned back to them, phone still in his hand. His face was suddenly stern and pensive. "Doctor, Miss Yuuki, I'm afraid I have to leave you now."

"That's all right. We'll clean up the meal for you."

"I appreciate that. Good-bye," he said with a nod, then practically sped out of the lounge.

"…I wonder what that was about."

"No idea…," Asuna said, turning to the window again.

Something about the sight of the escort ship gradually fading through the morning mist made her uneasy. Quietly, Asuna clenched her left hand.

CHAPTER NINE

Creak.

Creak.

With the repetition of each tiny sound, I felt my heart shrink.

The sound came from the tip of my still-unnamed black sword, which was just barely sticking into the gap between Central Cathedral's roughly one-inch-thick white marble blocks.

My right hand was damp with sweat where it clung to the sword's hilt, and my elbow and shoulder joints were screaming with pain, ready to disconnect at any moment. Which made sense—my assuredly not-beefy arm was supporting the weight of two people, one ultra-high-priority longsword, and a full set of armor.

There wasn't a single handhold in the mirrorlike smoothness of the wall, so there was no way for me to wedge the sword farther into the surface. There was nothing below me but an endless expanse. And in addition to the pain in my right hand, my left was also reaching its limit as it clung to the lady knight in her heavy suit of golden armor.

Physical fatigue in the Underworld was slightly different from in the real world. In terms of long-distance walking, sprinting, fierce training, and lifting heavy objects, it was the same sensation. The difference was that fatigue acted like injury in the way that it reduced one's "life," the numerical value of vitality in the Underworld—i.e., your hit points.

In the real world, hardly anyone ever literally died of fatigue. Before the body could reach a state of serious, permanent injury, fatigue rendered you unable to move. But here, it was possible at times for strength of will to override physical possibility. In other words, it was theoretically possible that you could run, resisting pain and exhaustion, until the moment your life reached zero and you instantly died.

At the moment, I was supporting an unbelievable amount of weight with my body. My life value was slowly but surely decreasing as long as this state continued. I could keep both hands clenched out of sheer determination, but eventually my life would reach zero, and I would die. In that instant, my hand would probably let go of the sword, and the knight with me would plunge to the ground hundreds of feet below and die as well.

I wasn't the only one suffering damage. My beloved sword was supporting more weight than it could handle, with only its very tip for leverage. And I'd already used the immensely taxing Perfect Weapon Control twice in the day's battles. I couldn't open its Stacia Window to check numbers, but I wouldn't be surprised if its life reached zero within a few minutes. When that happened, the sword would shatter and no longer recover its strength by merely returning to its sheath.

It would be a terrible shame to break my sword before I could even give it a name, not that it would matter for long once I plunged to my death. I needed to do something and fast, but just holding on took all my strength, plus…

"That's enough! Let go of me!" shrieked the woman dangling from me—Alice Synthesis Thirty, the golden Integrity Knight with the Osmanthus Blade. "I would rather die than live with the shame of having been saved by a criminal sinner like you!"

She struggled and rocked, trying to break herself loose from my grip. Her gauntlet slipped a little bit in my sweaty palm.

"Arghk…stahppit…" I tried to control the shaking while uttering nonsense. But the vibration of her thrashing worked the blade's tip a tiny millimeter out of the wall. When all was still again, I glanced down and yelled, "Stop moving, idiot! You're an Integrity Knight; you should know that getting suicidal here isn't going to solve anything! Idiot!"

"Wha…?" The pale face visible between my feet turned red. "Y-you…you dare insult me, you rogue? Take that back!"

"Shut up! I'm calling you an idiot because you *are* an idiot, you idiot! Idiot!" I yelled, uncertain whether I was doing this to engage her in negotiating for help, or whether I was just working out my frustration. "Do you understand the situation? If you fall off and die here, Eugeo's going to keep climbing up to Administrator's chamber all by himself! It's supposed to be your job to stop that from happening! Shouldn't your top priority as an Integrity Knight be to sacrifice anything you can to stop him?! If you're too stupid to see the logic there, then you're an idiot!!"

"Th-that's *eight* times you have insulted me now…," Alice said, glaring up at me with her cheeks reddening; I doubted she'd ever been called an idiot since she became an Integrity Knight. She raised her Osmanthus Blade, eliciting chills as I pictured an attack that would send us both to our doom. But it seemed that her sense of reason won out, because the sword soon dangled at her side again.

"I see. There is a logic to what you say," she admitted, her pearly teeth gritted. "But why don't you let go?! Can you prove that your reason is not pity, a fate more painful than death?!"

It certainly wasn't pity. Saving Alice from this fate was half the reason Eugeo and I were here at Central Cathedral in the first place. But there wasn't enough time to explain all that. And besides, it wasn't Alice Synthesis Thirty that Eugeo wanted to rescue from the tower, but his childhood friend Alice Zuberg, who had been abducted from Rulid Village eight years ago.

I tried to come up with an argument that would convince Alice as I fought against the screaming pain. But no such rationale manifested. I could offer up only a partial truth.

"I…Eugeo and I didn't come charging up the cathedral for the purpose of destroying the Axiom Church."

I stared down at Alice's fierce blue eyes, searching for the right words. "We want to protect the realm from a Dark Territory invasion, just like you. We fought a goblin band in the mountains two years ago…not that I expect you to believe me. So I don't want you to die, if you're one of the most powerful Integrity Knights. You're a valuable source of power."

She drew her brows together, taken aback by this comment, but regained her poise to snap, "Then why do you turn your sword upon your fellow man and commit the greatest taboo of bloodshed?!"

The question came from a place of pure righteousness—implanted by Administrator for her own ends or not. Alice's eyes burned. "Why did you harm Eldrie Synthesis Thirty-One and all those subsequent knights?!"

Sadly, I didn't have a convincing reply. My desire to save the human realm was both honest intent and an act of hypocrisy. If I reached the top of the cathedral and defeated Administrator, Cardinal would regain all system privileges. In order to prevent the coming catastrophe, she would attempt to reinitialize the entire Underworld. And as of that moment, I couldn't think of a way to avoid this outcome: salvation through utter oblivion.

But if Alice and I plunged to our deaths, that would only make the coming tragedy worse. If the "final stress test"—an invasion from the Dark Territory—happened without Cardinal having control, the Integrity Knights and Administrator would fall in battle, and every last human being would be agonizingly slaughtered.

The worst part of all was knowing that if I died here, I would simply wake up in a Soul Translator somewhere in the real world. The Underworldians would perish in a hell of suffering, and I would be perfectly fine back in reality. An unthinkable conclusion.

"I'm..."

With the little time I had left, what could I possibly say that would convince the protector of the church and its dedication to order? But no matter how futile, there was nothing else I could do in this situation.

"Eugeo and I attacked Raios Antinous and Humbert Zizek at the academy because the Axiom Church and Taboo Index are wrong. Deep down, you know that's true, don't you? Just because the Taboo Index doesn't outlaw it, should higher nobles be allowed to torment and defile completely innocent girls like Ronie and Tiese...? Is that what you believe?!"

My body shook as my mind flashed back to the scene I witnessed two years ago in the student dorm—the girls mercilessly trussed up with tears in their eyes. The tip of the sword creaked in the wall again, but I barely noticed it.

"Well?! Answer me, Integrity Knight!!"

My raging emotions manifested in a hot droplet that spilled from my eye to Alice's forehead below. The golden knight sucked in a sharp breath, her eyes gaping. When her trembling lips opened again, it seemed as though the harshness of her attitude had given way to something else.

"The law…is the law. Sin…is sin. If the people are allowed to define the law by their own needs, then how are we to uphold order in the world?"

"And who decides if Administrator was right to create the law that way? The god of the celestial realm? Why aren't I being fried by a bolt of lightning from above, then?!"

"Because Stacia's will is made clear through the actions of us, her servants!"

"And Eugeo and I came up all this way hoping to clear that up! We want to defeat Administrator and prove that it's a mistake! And for the exact same reason…"

I glanced up briefly at the sword wedged into the wall and saw that it was nearly out. One move from Alice, one tiny little gust of wind, and the tip would either break or fall out, sending us plunging below.

"…I refuse to let you die right now!!"

I sucked in the biggest breath I could, tensed my stomach, and summoned all my remaining willpower.

"Yaaaah!!" I bellowed, yanking my left arm up to lift Alice. Both arms and shoulders screamed with pain, but I managed to bring her up to my level and use the last bits of my strength to shout, "Stick your sword in that seam! I can't hold out… please!"

Up close, her features were twisted with emotion. A moment later, she lifted her arm and loudly, deeply thrust her Osmanthus Blade into the seam between marble blocks. At nearly the same second, my black sword slipped out of the stone, and my other hand lost the grip holding Alice.

In a single, vivid instant of panic from head to toe, I envisioned my long, long fall to the ground, and the oblivion that awaited.

But all I actually felt was a split second of floating, then a fierce tugging shock. Alice's hand had shot out and grabbed the back of my shirt collar. Once I was sure she was supporting all my weight with her sword and arms, I let out a deep breath. My pounding heart gradually eased to a state less than sheer panic.

"..."

I looked up at her. In the span of a single second, we had switched positions both physically and mentally. The golden Integrity Knight clenched her jaw, as if grappling with every possible kind of conflicting emotion. I felt her fingers loosen and tighten over and over, shifting pressure on the back of my collar.

Eugeo was the only Underworldian I knew who could be uncertain under such extreme circumstances. The other artificial fluctlights, for better or for worse, were blindly faithful to a certain set of behaviors, and did not need to grapple with huge, difficult choices. Put another way, all the truly important decisions were always handed down to them by something or someone else.

In other words, Alice the Integrity Knight's mind had a more "human" quality than many of her fellow Underworldians—even after her soul had been altered by Administrator.

I had no way of knowing what sort of inner debate she housed. But after several seconds that felt like an unfathomable eternity, she easily lifted my body up to its former level.

Unlike her, I had no reason to hesitate. I instantly thrust my sword into the seam once more, exhaling. Once I was stable again, Alice withdrew her hand from my collar and turned her face away. Despite the sternness of her words, her voice itself was weak and small.

"...I did not save you, only repaid what you did for me. Besides...we have not finished our duel."

"Ah, I see...In that case, we're even now," I said, choosing my words carefully. "Here's a suggestion. Both of us need to find a way to get back into the tower. So why don't we call a truce until then?"

"…A truce?" she asked, turning to throw me a truly mistrustful glance.

"Yes. I doubt we can manage to destroy the cathedral's wall again, and it won't be easy to climb it. If we work together, it will raise our chances of survival. Of course, if you've got any easy ways back inside, I'm all ears."

"…"

She bit her lip in frustration. "If such a method existed, I would have done it already."

"Yeah. Obviously. So may I assume we're in agreement on a truce and cooperation?"

"Before I say yes…what exactly do you mean by cooperation?"

"If one of us seems likely to fall, the other helps. If we had a rope, it would make it easier for us to maintain our position, but I suppose that's asking too much."

The knight did not answer or look at me for a long time, then bobbed her head almost imperceptibly. "It is a logical suggestion… I must admit. I suppose I have no better choice," she said, turning to glare at me. "But the instant we return to the tower interior, I will cut you down. Do not forget this inevitable outcome."

"I'll…keep it in mind."

She nodded with satisfaction, then cleared her throat, signaling a topic change. "So…you mentioned needing a rope? Do you have any extra fabric?"

"Fabric…?"

I looked down at my outfit, realizing I didn't have so much as a handkerchief in my pockets. If this were good old Alfheim, I could produce a veritable ton of extra clothes, capes, and so on from my virtual item storage, but the Underworld was not blessed with such convenience.

"…Well, all I've got is this shirt and these pants. If need be, I'll take them off, though," I offered with a one-shouldered shrug.

Alice made the bitterest face I'd ever seen and yelled, "That will not be necessary! You must be joking. I cannot believe you would head into battle with nothing but a sword."

"Hey, you dragged me and Eugeo here from the academy with nothing but the clothes on our backs, right?"

"But you snuck into the tower's armory, didn't you? There were plenty of very fine ropes in there that...oh, forget it. This is a waste of time," she snorted, turning away. She lifted her right hand in its golden gauntlet, then grimaced when she realized she couldn't take her other hand off the sword hilt.

She thrust her arm toward me and commanded, "Undo the fastener on my gauntlet with your free hand."

"Huh?"

"And do not touch my skin under any circumstances. Quickly now!"

"..."

From what Eugeo told me, back in Rulid, Alice had been a bright, friendly, and kind girl to all. So where was this totally opposite personality coming from?

At last, the feeling was back in my left hand. I lifted it up to the fastener on her gauntlet. I held the metal device so she could pull her hand free. Her pale, slender fingers made a gesture, and she shouted, "System Call!"

This was followed by some complex, unfamiliar commands. The gauntlet in my hand flashed and began to change shape. Within a few seconds, I had a beautiful, coiled golden chain in my hand.

"Whoa...a matter-transformation spell...?"

"Weren't you listening? Are those ears on the sides of your head, or carnivorous holes for devouring insects? That was just a shape-changing art. Only the pontifex herself can perform the art of altering the very material."

I apologized to Alice, who clearly didn't view our truce as a chance to soften her tone, then tested the strength of the chain. I stuck the end into my mouth and tugged; it felt like my teeth were going to pop out. The metal was thinner than my pinkie finger, but it was clearly tough enough, and the chain was book-ended with sturdy-looking fasteners.

I stuck one of the fasteners onto my belt and held out the other end, which Alice took and attached to the metal clasp of her sword belt. The length of hanging chain between us ran about fifteen feet long. As long as we didn't both fall at the same time, this gave us some measure of security.

"All right..."

I glanced around to survey our situation. Based on the placement of the sun, we were hanging from the western wall of Central Cathedral. The sky overhead was turning from blue to purple, while the sunlight hitting the white stone painted it a soft orange hue. I estimated it was about half past three.

After a very careful glance past my feet and the thin wisps of cloud beyond them, I could make out the stone walls that surrounded the cathedral garden like a miniature play set, then the rest of Centoria, split into four by the Everlasting Walls. The sight was a reminder of the impossible height of the tower.

Counting the thickness of the stone partitions, I estimated each floor of the tower to be about twenty feet high, so the height of the eightieth floor, where I fought Alice, would be over fifteen hundred feet off the ground—perhaps more like sixteen or seventeen, given the high ceiling on the fiftieth floor. If I fell from here, there was no chance of survival. My body would be so pulverized by the impact that I'd be reduced to dust. The air around us was gentle for now, but there was no guarantee it wouldn't blow harder.

I shivered and clenched the hilt of my sword tighter, then wiped the sweat from my free palm on my pants.

"So, uh...just so I'm clear on this...," I started to say.

Alice's face shot up to look at me; she'd been gazing down as well. I thought she looked a bit paler than before, but her tone of voice was just as blunt as ever. "What?"

"I was just wondering...if you know the high-level sacred arts to change the shape of items, maybe you'd also be privy to an art to…fly? Okay, sorry, forget I asked," I stammered at the sight of her arched eyebrow.

"Did you learn *anything* in school?" she snapped. "The only person in the entire world who can fly in midair is the pontifex herself. Even the youngest apprentice monk knows that!"

"Hey, I said I was just checking! You don't have to get so mad at me."

"I did not appreciate your insinuation!"

It was becoming more clear by the moment that Alice the Integrity Knight and I were simply not designed to get along on a personal level. Still, I stifled my urge to snap back and asked, "Fine…so in that case…is it possible to call that enormous dragon you flew me here on?"

"It's just one stupid question after another. Dragons are only allowed to approach the thirtieth-floor landing. Even Uncle…er, the knights' commander himself isn't allowed to take his dragon higher than that."

"H-how would I know those rules?!"

"You ought to have realized the implication, since the landing was placed only on the thirtieth floor!" she said, glaring at me yet again for a good three seconds before we both turned away in a huff. I spent the next three seconds calming my rage over her totally unfair accusations before I was ready to resume.

"So…there's no way for us to escape this predicament through the air…"

It took Alice another couple of seconds to regain her cool. Her blue eyes caught mine. "Not even birds can approach the upper reaches of the cathedral. The pontifex cast some kind of special art unknown to me that prevents them from coming closer."

"I see…Very thorough."

Off in the far distance, I saw a birdlike shape, but it didn't seem to be getting any closer. I supposed it was some combination of Administrator's magical power and a pathological sense of caution. In a sense, the abnormal height of this structure was both a symbol of power and an indication of fear toward some unseen foe.

"So that leaves three options…climb down, climb up, or break through the wall again."

"The third will be difficult. Central Cathedral's walls possess a nearly infinite life and regenerative ability, just like the Everlasting Walls. The same can be said of the glass windows on the lower levels."

"So we can't even climb down to where the windows are," I murmured. She nodded.

"In fact, that hole punctured in the wall is even difficult for me to believe…I suppose I must accept it as some freakishly unlucky outcome from melding our Perfect Weapon Control arts, so it produced a huge burst of power. You have really been a thorn in my side."

"…"

I merely breathed through my nostrils, certain that arguing my case would only lead us into another downward spiral. "In that case…couldn't we repeat the phenomenon if we attempted the same thing again?"

"I can't rule out the possibility…but it would be difficult to make our way through the wall in the few seconds before it repairs itself again, and more importantly…I've already used the Perfect Weapon Control of my Osmanthus Blade twice. It needs either a good helping of sunlight or a long rest in my sheath before I can use it again."

"True, the same goes for mine. It needs a few hours of sheath time…and I'm sure that just hanging from it like this is doing plenty of damage on its own. Whether we go up or down, we should probably start moving soon."

I brushed the marble stone with my free hand. It was devastatingly smooth. The blocks were nearly six feet to a side, stacked upon one another infinitely, with not even a window to break the totality of the west face. And even those were indestructible, according to Alice.

Our only means of traversing the tower side was to utilize something like rock-climbing hooks that we could jam into the seams of the marble stone to use as handholds. The amount of energy required to go up or down seemed about the same, so I figured we might as well go up, but that led to another major problem.

I gave Alice my most serious face, preparing for another nonanswer, and asked, "If we go up from here...will there be a spot we could use to get back inside the tower?"

As expected, Alice looked hesitant at first. She bit her lip. If there was a place farther up to reenter the building, it would have to be very close to the top floor, where Administrator lived. It would be tantamount to taboo for an Integrity Knight tasked with protecting the Church to escort an enemy to such a vital place.

But Alice drew a deep breath and said firmly, "There will be. On the ninety-fifth floor, in a place called the Morning Star Lookout, the tower is open to the air, with only pillars for support. If we can climb up that far, it will be easy to get back in. However..."

Her crystal-blue eyes got even harder. "If we actually make it up to the ninety-fifth floor, I will have to kill you."

There was enough force in her gaze to make the back of my neck tingle. I nodded. "That was the deal, I believe. So shall we climb the wall, then?"

"...Very well. It's more practical than going all the way down to the ground from here...But you make it sound so simple. How will we climb such a sheer wall?"

"Why, we'll just run vertically right up it...I'm kidding," I added hastily, seeing the temperature in her eyes rapidly dropping to subzero numbers. I cleared my throat, switched hands on the sword, and motioned with my free hand. "System Call! Generate Metallic Element!"

A shining metal-gray light appeared, which took further shape as my command continued. It grew out to a good foot and a half with a pointed end—a brand-new climbing hook.

I gripped it tight, looked up at the seam in the stone where my sword was stuck, and pulled my arm back.

"Hmph!"

With all the strength I could muster, I drove the hook into the wall. To my relief, it didn't break. The blade stuck right in the narrow crack. I gave it a few firm yanks up and down as a test, and it appeared wedged tightly enough to support my weight.

Objects generated by sacred arts had very little life and would disappear in a matter of hours if just left around. So it wasn't suitable to be a lifeline between Alice and me, but it would at least be sturdy enough to act as a decent foothold when climbing the wall.

I could feel the doubt in Alice's gaze as I held the hook tight with my right hand and pried loose my poor abused sword with my left. Once it was safely back in its sheath, I hung from the fifteen-inch support with both hands and kicked up like mounting a bar.

My physical abilities in the Underworld weren't exactly like in the later days of *SAO*, where I had agility that would make a B-movie ninja jealous, but I was still much nimbler and stronger than in the real world. I put my right foot on the bar and rose up to a standing position, with my left hand pressed firmly against the wall.

"A-are you all right?" came a hoarse voice. I saw Alice looking up at me with a pale face and her free hand clutching the golden chain. She looked surprisingly young and innocent. For a moment, I was tempted to pretend to fall, just to see what she'd do, but then thought better of it.

"I think...I am."

I gave her a little wave with my right hand, then chanted another sacred art to summon a fresh climbing hook. I drove it into the next seam overhead and climbed up as before. It was only six feet of progress, but I felt a small measure of accomplishment at the success.

I called down to Alice, "I think this will work! Just follow me and climb up on the first bar below."

The Integrity Knight stared at me without budging. Eventually her lips moved, and I just barely heard the sound, "...an't."

"Huh? What'd you say?"

"I said...*I can't*!"

"Uh...sure you can. With your strength, it should be easy to pull yourself up to—"

"That's not what I mean!" she insisted, cutting off my awkward

attempt at a pep talk. "I have never experienced a situation like this before…and at the risk of exposing myself to shame, it is all I can do just to hang here. I simply can't climb up on such a slender step…"

Her voice trailed off into nothing again.

I was shocked. As a general rule, Underworldians were uncomfortable with situations outside their personal experience or expectations. So they had a poor ability to react to impossible circumstances, to the extent that when I cut off his arms, Raios's fluctlight actually collapsed before his life ran out—or so I assumed.

Even an Integrity Knight had to be struggling with the experience of breaking a hole through a supposedly indestructible wall, getting sucked into the void outside, and dangling from a height that even dragons couldn't reach. Perhaps though, deep down, the superlative sword-wielding Alice Synthesis Thirty was just another girl.

In any case, given her abundance of pride, I had to assume that the Integrity Knight's admission of weakness meant she was at her wits' end.

"Okay!" I shouted. "Then I'll pull you up to the bar with the chain!"

Alice bit her lip, apparently weighing fear against pride, and ultimately decided that she'd cast her lot already and wasn't going to change her mind. She tugged on the chain.

"Th-thank you for the assistance," she squeaked. I gripped the chain, resisting the urge to tease her.

"All right, I'll lift you slowly. Here goes."

I carefully pulled it up. The hook under my feet creaked, but it seemed to be able to withstand two people for a bit of time. I lifted the golden knight a few feet, careful not to rock the foothold too much, then held the chain in midair.

"There. You can pull out your sword now."

Alice nodded, slowly removing the point of the Osmanthus Blade from the white stone. A large amount of fresh weight yanked on the chain, and I gritted my teeth as I held it still. Once her sword was back in its sheath, I resumed lifting.

When Alice's boots were resting on the first hook below, I

instructed her, "Now place both your hands against the wall to steady yourself…good. I'm releasing the chain now."

I couldn't see her face due to the angle, but she did subtly tip her head as she clung to the wall. Imagining her desperate expression below that windswept blond hair, I lowered my right arm. She momentarily wobbled, then regained her balance.

"Phew…"

I let out a long breath I didn't realize I'd been holding.

How many more feet until this so-called Morning Star Lookout on the ninety-fifth floor? As long as I could successfully repeat this process, we would make it eventually. The problem boiled down to the time it took to make it up one block. Night would fall eventually, and if we needed to sleep while hanging off the wall.

"Okay, I'm going to go one step higher again," I warned her.

She turned her panicked face toward me and replied, barely audible through the breeze, "Please be careful."

"Sure thing."

I gave her a bracing thumbs-up—a gesture I was certain no one in the Underworld understood—then chanted the system command for a third climbing hook.

Despite Centoria getting ready for its summer solstice festival in the lands below us, when the sun began sinking, its progress was mercilessly swift. Against the white stone, the orange light of the setting sun quickly progressed from a burning red to violet to deep navy blue, until only fragments of the End Mountains were visible in the last red light of the day, far, far to the west.

Overhead, the stars were twinkling, but they did not bless our progress. An hour earlier, we had come across an unexpected limitation of the system that was proving rather difficult.

The process of our climb was simple: I created a hook with sacred arts, stuck it in the gap between the marble blocks, and climbed on top of it. Then I would lift Alice with the chain so that she stood on the hook below me. Once we did this about ten times, we'd gotten a single repetition down to under three minutes.

The problem was with generating the hooks themselves. There was no statistic in this world that corresponded to what we'd call *mana points* in *ALO*. The magic they called *sacred arts* could be repeated as often as you wanted, as long as the spell was within your system access level.

That did not mean they were usable anywhere and everywhere, however. This world's rules dictated that all production required magical resources, a fact that applied to sacred arts as much as anything else. In order to execute an art, you needed to expend spatial resources, either in the vicinity of the user or through consuming the life of valuable catalysts or living things—even humans.

Spatial resources were tricky because they couldn't be measured in numbers. For the most part, this value came from sunlight or the earth. Wherever the ground was fertile and open to the sun, resources would be rich, enough to support continued casting of high-level arts. On the other end, a windowless room in a stone building would run out of resources very quickly and take a long time to recharge.

By those rules, our current situation—stuck at a height of fifteen hundred feet off the ground with the sun sinking over the horizon—was about as bad as it could possibly get. Before long, my hook-generating sacred arts had dried up all of the twilight's resources, leaving us unable to continue upward.

"System Call! Generate Metallic Element!"

Over my palm, outstretched to catch some last bit of light in vain, a few little motes of silver light floated, then snuffed out with tiny wisps of smoke.

I sighed, and below me, I heard Alice murmur, "Generating containers like that uses much spiritual power. Now that Solus is gone, you'll be lucky to manage one per hour. How far have we climbed?"

"Err…I think we're past the eighty-fifth floor now."

"So there's a long way to go until ninety-five."

I gazed longingly at the traces of purple in the sky. "Yeah…and in any case, once it's dark, it'll be too dangerous to keep climbing. And if we try to camp out here, getting any rest will be difficult…"

At worst, someone would need to dangle from the chain, but

not only could we not create more hooks, they would also disappear after a few dozen minutes, so we'd have no choice but to use our swords as supports again. And I wasn't sure they could withstand the pressure all night.

I looked up the wall face, stubbornly hoping that there'd be *some* kind of outcropping we could connect the chain to, using its fastener. And then…

"Oh…"

There was a series of evenly spaced shadows with complex shapes against the wall not much more than twenty feet above us. When the sun went down, the mist around the tower dissipated, revealing these hidden decorations.

"Hey…does that look like something to you?" I asked, pointing. Alice looked up and narrowed her blue eyes.

"You're right…Statues, perhaps? But why would they be here, so high up, where no one will see them?"

"I don't care why, as long as we can sit and rest on them. But they're a good…eight mels above us. We'll need another three bars in order to climb up there."

"Three bars…," she repeated, deep in thought. "All right. I was planning to save this for an emergency…and it looks like the time has come."

She pushed her back against the wall and removed the gauntlet on her left hand. She stared at the faintly glowing piece of armor and began to chant the command for a sacred art. When she finished her execution (many times smoother than mine), there was a flash, and the gauntlet had turned into three more climbing hooks. Alice's matter-transforming arts must've had better energy efficiency than generating from thin air, given my inability to summon any myself.

"Here, use these," she said, stretching upward with the hooks in her hand. I crouched down and carefully took the tools.

"Thank you—this is a huge help."

"If it's truly necessary, I have more armor…"

I glanced at the fine breastplate that covered her upper half and shook my head. "No...we'll leave that one to the very end. You never know what we might need..."

I carefully got to my feet, stuck two of the hooks into my belt, and lifted the third.

"*Uraa!*"

Sure enough, the golden hook was much sturdier than the metallic elements I'd created; it sank deep into the rock's seam. I did the now-familiar climbing routine and used the chain to pull Alice up. After another repetition, the mysterious objects were half as far away, and much clearer in the darkness.

They were stone statues, as it turned out; large and ornate, a significant number surrounded the cathedral walls on narrow terraces. But these were not the holy statues of goddesses and angels that I'd seen inside the tower. They were human-shaped, true, but bent at the knees into a crouch, with their arms folded menacingly over their legs. Gnarled muscles bulged, and wings as sharp as knives extended from their backs.

Worst of all, the heads of the statues were utterly alien, curved and elongated at the front and ending in a conical mouth. They looked like the heads of some kind of grotesque giant weevils.

"Ugh...that's such a creepy design," I groaned.

"Huh...? W-wait...that's from the Dark Territory...!" Alice exclaimed.

Just then, the head of the statue right above me craned back and forth, its lamprey mouth opening and closing. That was not some decorative statue carved out of stone. It was...*alive.*

If this were a quest in some ordinary VRMMO back in the real world, a statue attack would be inevitable after a demonstration like that. But in this case, the person writing the scenario was either a total sadist or a green beginner. We were stuck on these foot-long hooks jammed into a sheer wall, with nowhere else to go.

The term *certain-defeat event* crossed my mind, but I dismissed it just as quick. This wouldn't be one of those thrill-ride incidents where someone would swoop in and save us if we fell. We had to use our brains to evade danger on our own, or we would die.

While I prepared myself for danger, the winged statue shook itself and began to change color. Its white skin, the same hue as the tower stone, began turning a slick charcoal black, starting from the extremities.

I drew my sword in anticipation of the black wings snapping out into full extension. Without taking my eyes off the former statue, I shouted down to Alice, "Looks like we'll have to fight here. Not falling off should be the top priority!"

But I didn't hear the Integrity Knight respond right away. I glanced down and saw her face, pale in the night, a perfect picture of shock. On the updraft of wind I heard the whisper: "No, how is this possible?"

An Integrity Knight should know everything about the Axiom Church. Why would she be so surprised? From what I knew through my secondhand reports about Administrator, she was abnormally cautious. Surely, it wasn't so unthinkable that she would not only prevent flight to the tower's upper sections, but also place stone guardians along the walls in case any challengers were persistent and mad enough to climb all the way.

The guardian—which, aside from the head, looked similar to a typical video game gargoyle—gripped the terrace ledge with clawed hands and emitted a whoosh of air from its mouth.

A shiver went down my back as I realized the gargoyles on either side of the animated one were also changing color. If they were placed equally around all four walls of the cathedral, there could be at least a hundred.

"Oh, damn," I hissed, turning to press my back to the wall and hefting up my sword. Just that was enough to unbalance me, given the tiny bar I was standing on. Even in *SAO*, I had never tried to fight like this.

But before I could even start planning, I heard the wings flapping overhead. The gargoyle was hovering against the dark-blue sky, the round eyes on either side of its elongated head fixed on me. The monster was bigger than I'd expected, probably more than six feet. Even its dangling tail looked about as long as I was tall.

"Bshaaa!!"

It let out a hiss like steam escaping a valve, then plunged head-first toward me.

It didn't seem to have any ranged attacks, fortunately, so I anticipated claws on one of its limbs to appear next. Right or left, top or bottom—

"...Whoa!!"

With a whiplike crack, its tail shot out. I jerked my head away and yelped in surprise; the tip grazed my cheek, as sharp and pointed as a knife.

I'd managed to dodge, but my balance was now a problem. I wobbled atop the hook, attempting to stay upright. Mercilessly, the gargoyle's tail shot at me again.

With my left hand against the wall to steady myself, I blocked the tail attack with the sword in my right. It was all I could do to hold it up like a shield. There was no way I could actually swing it around to sever the spike.

"Urgh..."

Sensing that this wasn't the time to be thrifty, I took my left hand off the wall and pulled out one of the two golden hooks in my belt. Envisioning the movements of the Throwing Weapons skill I'd practiced so much in *SAO*, I hurled the spear at the center of the gargoyle's body.

I didn't put that much effort into the throw, but the short spear lived up to its nature as Alice's gauntlet, shining bright through the gloom to sink deep into the gargoyle's lower stomach.

"Bshhi!" it hissed, its circular mouth spurting black blood. The monster flapped its wings irregularly, trying to regain altitude. I'd inflicted some good damage, but not enough to vanquish it. The black, insectoid eyes glared at me with rage.

Even knowing there were more important things at hand, I couldn't help but wonder, Was it just a program controlling that freakish monster? Or, like the people from the Dark Territory, was it an artificial fluctlight...?

"Bshhhuuu!!"

A second cry jolted me out of that thought. Two more gargoyles had descended from the terrace and were circling around, waiting for their opportunity to strike.

"Alice, draw your sword! The monsters are coming for you!"

I glanced below and saw that the Integrity Knight was not yet over her unexplained shock. If they attacked now, she'd be either skewered by a tail or knocked off the hook.

Should I try to climb the remaining dozen or so feet to the terrace while the gargoyles are still hanging back? I had only one hook left in my belt—and I suspected the furious beast with the hook stuck in its stomach would not be kind enough to give it back.

If the current high-pitched screech was any indication, the three hissing monsters were getting ready to attack again. I could potentially be forced to let go of the lifeline chain and jump down onto a gargoyle if it swooped on Alice. I felt my belt for the chain's clasp. Then my eyes went wide.

The length of the chain was over fifteen feet. And there were only about twelve feet between me and the ledge.

"Alice...Alice!!" I bellowed as I slid my sword back into its sheath. The Integrity Knight twitched and turned her blue eyes to me at last.

"Hold tight to the chain!"

She frowned, looking confused. I used both hands to grip the chain connected to her sword sheath and pulled, lifting her off the hook. She belatedly grabbed the chain and gasped, "Wait... are you...?"

"If we both survive, I'll give you all the apologies you want later!!"

I sucked in a deep breath, then yanked—no, hurled—the knight hanging on the chain upward. Her long golden hair and white skirt billowed through the air as Alice swung in a semicircle.

"Eyaaaa!!" she shrieked, a surprisingly amateur reaction, as she passed between the gargoyles on her way to landing on the ledge above. *Landing* not in the active sense, but the passive. I decided to ignore the very unladylike *Murgk!* that ended her scream.

The exertion of my wild throw hurtled me off the hook I had been balancing on. If Alice didn't hold firm up on the ledge to support my weight, we'd both plunge off the side of the building.

Thankfully, the Integrity Knight sensed what needed to be done: She grabbed the chain with both hands and dug in her feet, although the first brief moment of weightlessness sent a shiver down my back.

"Why...youuuuuu!!" she raged, pulling as hard as she could. Just as Alice had, I flew through the air, and though the impact of my back slamming against the marble wall knocked the breath from my lungs, I'd never been as relieved as when I felt the terrace floor under my feet. I could've lain there on the flat surface forever, until Alice kicked me in the ribs.

"Wh-what in the world were you thinking, you madman?!"

"I didn't have a better choice to...We can talk later! Here they come!"

I drew my weapon again and pointed the tip at the gargoyle trio rising toward us. With what little time we had before combat resumed, I looked left and right to get a grasp of the arena.

The high-wire circus act we'd executed to get up there granted us a ledge about three feet wide around the building. There was no decoration, just flat, simple marble jutting horizontally out of the tower wall. In fact, it literally served as a shelf, and it occurred to me that this was just meant to be a resting place for the gargoyles.

Since Alice hadn't known about the terrace, I maintained hope that there might be some special door or window along the wall nearby, but sadly, there was nothing. The only features in sight were the other monstrous statues that hadn't come to life yet, lined up all the way down to the corners of the building. It was a horrifying thing to see, but fortunately the only ones currently active were the three flying up toward us.

With her confidence returned from being on solid ground, Alice slid her Osmanthus Blade from its sheath. But that hadn't solved all her questions. "Yes, I'm sure of it," she rasped. "But why...would they be here...?"

The gargoyles were back on our level again, but they were keeping their distance, wary of our weapons. Without taking my eyes off the hovering creatures, I asked Alice, "What has been bothering you? Do you know something about those monsters?"

"...Yes...I do," she replied, to my surprise. "They're wicked beasts that serve the evil sorcerers of the Dark Territory that created them. We know them to be called *minions*. It is a word in the sacred tongue that means *follower* or *subordinate*."

"Minions...Well, I can tell they're from the Dark Territory based on their looks—but why would they be lined up on the walls of the holiest place in the world?"

"That's what I want to know!" Alice grunted. She bit her lip. "Obviously, they should not be here. It's inconceivable that these minions would cross the End Mountains without attracting notice, converge on Centoria, only to fly this high and land on Central Cathedral itself. And..."

"And it's *completely* impossible that someone powerful within the Church might have intentionally placed them there...?" I asked, filling in the blank. Alice shot me a nasty look but did not offer a rebuttal.

I looked at the gargoyles hovering close by and asked, "Just tell me one thing. Are those minions intelligent? Do they understand human words?"

Alice shook her head. "That would truly be impossible. Minions are not living things like goblins or orcs. They are agents without souls, created by sorcerers who worship the god of darkness, Vecta. The only things they understand are a few simple commands from their master."

"...Ah," I said, breathing a secret sigh of relief. I knew that I was overlooking the present danger, but I still couldn't help but feel resistance at the thought of killing a being with the same kind of fluctlight as a human.

Cardinal had told me that babies were born only to men and women whose marriages had been ratified by the Axiom Church—probably because they had the particular system command that executed it. The denizens of the Dark Territory had to work the same way. Therefore, the minions generated by dark arts would run on the same program code as wild animals, rather than artificial fluctlights.

With that in mind, the hostility I sensed from those insectoid eyes had the same kind of digital fakeness that I'd experienced with so many monsters in the *SAO* days. Something in their routine switched from *hang back* to *attack*, and they beat their wings and rose in unison.

"Here they come!" I shouted, holding up my sword. The minion with the golden rod stuck in its chest swooped toward me first, thanks to the accumulated hate value.

This time, it started by swiping at me with its claws rather than its tail. It wasn't particularly fast, but it'd been so long since I'd fought a monster that it was hard to judge the distances involved. I was focused on blocking the claws, waiting for a good opening to strike, when, out of the corner of my eye, I caught sight of the other two descending on Alice.

"Watch out—the other two are going for you!" I warned.

"Who in the world do you think I am?" she snapped, holding the Osmanthus Blade at her left side.

With a tremendous slice, the golden blade flashed outward, practically lighting up the night. It wasn't a feint or a combination attack, just a single, medium-height slash: In the Aincrad style, it would be known as Horizontal. But it was so fast and devastating that I could feel a subconscious cold sweat break out on my skin from standing next to it. The utter perfection of this single attack had me entirely overmatched, with no room for defense or evasion, in our battle on the eightieth floor. My years of VRMMO life had turned me into a permanent proponent of combination attacks, but her single attack had absolutely crushed that conviction.

Alice paused at the end of her swing, and the four arms of the minions toppled off. Even their trunks, which were well out of her sword range, silently separated across the chest.

The monsters toppled without even a death scream, filthy black blood spurting from the clean-cut stumps. Not a single drop so much as touched Alice, of course. She straightened up, quite matter-of-fact, and looked over at me as I stood there struggling with defense.

"Do you need any help?"

"...N-no, I'll manage," I protested. I'd seen all of the minions' attacks now and sidestepped a claw-and-tail combination attack. Before the monster could pull away to a safe distance, I executed a familiar combo of my own.

For a long time, I found it mysterious that the Underworld had the same sword-skills concept as *SAO*. After two years of internal debate, I still hadn't arrived at a completely satisfying answer. Perhaps the Rath engineers utilized *SAO*'s Seed platform to build the foundation of their virtual world, but as far as I knew, The Seed didn't actually have the sword-skills function built in. If it did, I would've been able to use sword skills when I converted to *Gun Gale Online*.

Perhaps wise Cardinal in her hidden library knew the truth, but I didn't ask her when I had the chance. Cardinal knew that she and all other Underworldians were living in an experiment designed by Rath, a reality she grappled with deeply. I couldn't bring myself to make her confront the fact that everything she knew was a kind of artifice. And at this point, the reason that sword skills existed here wasn't that important. As long as they worked properly and were tools I could use, that was all that mattered.

The sword in my hand glowed blue and engaged in the four-part attack Horizontal Square.

"Rrraaaahh!" I bellowed. My sword lopped off the minion's arms and tail, then severed it clean across the chest with the final swipe, not that I was trying to compete with Alice. The momentum of the attack nearly took me off the ledge, but I managed to hold still in time, watching the pieces of the monster fall separately through the clouds below.

I figured that if the pieces didn't evaporate into thin air during the fall, some monk wandering the cathedral grounds below would eventually get a real scare.

"Ooooh," Alice murmured with the approval of a teacher observing her pupil's exhibition. I swiped my blade left and right before returning it to the sheath at my side—I'd have preferred to stash it over my back, but there were no shoulder harnesses in the armory—and looked at her sidelong. "What?"

"Nothing. It was a rather odd skill—that is all. I daresay you could attract quite a crowd if you exhibited it on a stage during the summer solstice festival."

"Gee, thanks."

I had to chuckle to myself from being with such a sardonic knight. Then a thought manifested, and I asked, "Have you ever even seen Centoria's solstice festival? If anything, it's a holiday for the common people. At Swordcraft Academy, hardly any of the upper noble children went to it..."

There were exceptions to the rule, of course; Sortiliena was a noble, and she looked forward to the festival every year, I recalled fondly.

Alice snorted. "Do not take me for one of those nobles with their airs. Of course...I...have...," she protested, before trailing off prematurely.

Her mouth was hanging open, her brow knitted in confusion, searching for some answer. She lifted her bare left hand and pressed her fingertips to her smooth forehead. Then she shook her head several times and mumbled, "No...One of the monks told me:...there was such a festival. Integrity Knights are forbidden... from mingling with the common folk...outside of duty..."

"..."

That made sense. The Integrity Knights believed they were summoned from Heaven by their pontifex, but that wasn't true. Administrator brought human beings who excelled in wisdom or strength to the cathedral and performed a Synthesis Ritual that locked their memories away and turned them into knights. Therefore, if any knights wandered around the cities below, they might run across their former family, leading to chaos.

Alice was number thirty, making her the second-newest knight after Eldrie Synthesis Thirty-One, who'd been converted this spring. Logic dictated that she'd probably been synthesized within the past year as well, and yet she'd been taken from Rulid eight years ago—leaving a blank period of seven years.

What kind of life had Alice lived here during that time? Was she learning sacred arts as an apprentice sister? Did Administrator have her frozen as a prisoner the whole time?

Perhaps she had actually visited Centoria's summer solstice festival before being turned into a knight. Maybe that little scrap of conversation was peeling away at an old memory hidden behind her memory block...

If I kept asking her little questions about the solstice festival, perhaps I could cause her Piety Module to eject, the way it had with Eldrie. I opened my mouth to speak, only to quickly clamp it shut.

Cardinal had said it would take more than just removing the Piety Module from Alice the Knight to turn her back into Eugeo's friend Alice Zuberg. I needed the fragment of her "most precious memory," which Administrator had removed entirely. So if I removed Alice's module now, it would cause her to go entirely unconscious. I didn't want to do that, especially when there was no saying when the next enemy might attack.

And for one thing, Alice hadn't even blinked when she ran into Eugeo, her childhood friend for years back in Rulid. That indicated the comprehensiveness of her memory block. It was unlikely that a minor topic like the festival would dislodge the module, and it would probably backfire by making her more suspicious of me.

She watched me mulling this over, a questioning look on her face, then switched gears and said, "Minion blood brings disease with it. We must clean it off."

"Hmm? Oh..."

Alice pointed at me, and for the first time, I realized that a few drops of the monster's blood had landed on my left cheek. I was going to wipe off the foul-smelling liquid with my sleeve when she snapped, "Don't do that!"

Stunned, I had to wonder how many years it had been since someone scolded me that way.

"Ugh, why must all men be this way?" she lamented. "Don't you at least have a hand towel of some kind?"

I stuffed my hands into my trouser pockets. The right one was empty, and the left was stuffed with things that weren't a handkerchief. I had to sheepishly admit, "I don't have one…"

"…Forget it. Use this," she said, producing a white handkerchief from somewhere in her skirt and handing it to me with a look of disgust.

If she was going to treat me like a little boy, I might as well lift up her skirt and rub my cheeks on it, but I realized she could easily kill me for that. Instead, I gratefully accepted the lace-edged kerchief and carefully wiped my cheek. It took the minion's blood clean off, as if the fabric had some sacred art of cleansing cast upon it.

"Thank you very much," I said, resisting the urge to call her *teacher*. I tried to hand back the cloth, but she turned her head away and said, "You will clean that before you return it, or I will cut you in two."

Dark days ahead. *What could I possibly say to someone like this to avoid combat once we're back inside the tower, so that I can reunite with Eugeo?* I looked around, imagining my partner climbing the stairs inside. By then, the light was totally gone from the sky, replaced by twinkling stars. We'd defeated the minions, but there was no way to generate new climbing hooks until the moon rose and gave us its meager resources.

I stuck Alice's handkerchief in my pocket and examined the terrace. As long as we didn't get any closer to them, it seemed that the minion statues would remain in stone form along the wall. If I rushed up to it and swung my sword at a vital spot before it could fully transform into flesh, I could probably beat it, but there was nothing to be gained by exposing myself to that danger.

We'd just have to wait here for the next few hours while the moon rose. I was perfectly happy to sit down and rest for a while, but I wasn't sure that I could avoid angering Alice for that entire time. I decided to hold my tongue until I could think of a way to improve the mood of the testy Integrity Knight.

CHAPTER TEN

It's been so long, I've forgotten what being alone is like, Eugeo thought as he climbed the long stairs.

Since that summer day eight years ago when he'd watched as Alice was chained to a dragon's leg and taken away, Eugeo had lived a life consumed by swinging his ax in the woods, with his eyes, ears, and heart effectively closed off from the world. Everyone in the village, including his family, refused to discuss the Integrity Knight's arrest of the village elder's daughter, as though even acknowledging it was a taboo of its own. In fact, they'd even begun to shun Eugeo for having been close to her in the first place.

But just as the villagers avoided him, so did Eugeo avoid others, as well as his own memories of the incident. Unable to admit his weakness and cowardice, he descended into the murky swamp of resignation, hoping to ignore both his past and future.

But then, two years ago, a boy who wandered into the forest without a single possession to his name had found Eugeo and dragged him out of that bottomless swamp. They defeated a band of goblins together and cut down the Gigas Cedar, and the boy helped give Eugeo confidence and a purpose.

Throughout the journey from Rulid, through the town of Zakkaria, and at last to Centoria, where they trained at Swordcraft Academy, Kirito had always been at his side. They had even made their way into the Axiom Church's Central Cathedral—though not the way they had originally planned—and had overcome numerous obstacles to reach high into the tower. It was all because Eugeo's black-haired partner was there, guiding and encouraging him.

But just before they were going to reach the final floor, Kirito had vanished. In the midst of a terrible battle against Alice Synthesis Thirty, an Integrity Knight created by implanting false memories into his childhood friend, Alice Zuberg, Kirito and Alice's Perfect Weapon Control arts intertwined abnormally, blowing a hole in an exterior wall.

The two combatants were instantly sucked outside, and the hole repaired itself soon after. Eugeo did everything he could to punch another hole in the wall, but nothing his Blue Rose Sword or his most powerful flame-based attack arts could do would affect the marble.

Most likely the walls were under a permanent kind of self-repairing art. As far as Eugeo knew, that would be an enormously high-level skill, the first line of which he couldn't even imagine. So even if he managed to damage the wall at great pains, it would seal itself back up just as quickly. The only reason that hole had opened in the first place must have been because the power created by the mixture of Kirito's and Alice's arts had surpassed anything the caster of the wall-enhancing spell could have imagined.

On the other hand, if they had enough power to create the hole, they would surely find a way to survive being sucked through the wall. In particular, Kirito's transcendent ability to react to sudden circumstances was surely greater than even the Integrity Knights'. He would find a way to stop their fall. He was probably climbing that wall from the outside even now. And that meant Alice was, too.

In her current state, Alice was a steadfast protector of the Axiom Church, so it was hard to imagine her helping Kirito, but if he could climb the wall, she would at least follow. If Eugeo could meet up with him above, they'd have another chance to use the dagger Cardinal had given them.

With that thought in mind, Eugeo passed through the door on the south end of the Cloudtop Garden, the eightieth floor of the cathedral, and proceeded up the stairs. He had to fight off the feeling of loneliness and futility that crept up on him once he was alone.

He started off slow and cautious, ready for an attack at any moment, but there was no sign of anyone else on the eighty-first or eighty-second floors. To get to that point, they'd defeated nine knights in total: Eldrie with his Frostscale Whip, Deusolbert with his Conflagration Bow, the apprentices Fizel and Linel, Fanatio of the Heaven-Piercing Blade, and the Four Whirling Blades who followed her. But there was still the commander of the knights and someone called the prime senator left to deal with, not to mention Administrator herself.

It didn't seem likely that the pontifex, who was head of the Axiom Church and thus all of humanity, would appear directly, but the knights' commander and prime senator surely wouldn't allow him to get to the top of the tower undisturbed. So Eugeo focused all his energy as he went, Blue Rose Sword in hand. And yet, he couldn't keep his mind from straying to other things.

What were Kirito and Alice doing now? Was she chasing him as he tried to climb the cathedral? Or were they still fighting, hanging off the side of the wall? Could Kirito's unique charisma have actually caused the proud knight to stay her blade...?

Suddenly, Eugeo sensed an unfamiliar emotion welling in his heart. It made him recall the conflicted feeling he'd had a few hours ago, when he'd turned his blade on the fallen Integrity Knight Deusolbert.

When he'd realized that Deusolbert was the very man who had taken Alice away from Rulid all those years ago, hatred and rage had overtaken him, pushing Eugeo to end the knight once and for all. But Kirito had intervened, and Eugeo had felt a powerful sense of inferiority.

You wouldn't have just stood there, he thought. *You would have attacked that knight, consequences be damned, and found a way to save Alice.*

Maybe Kirito's strength and kindness would find a way into Alice's heart. This Alice was an imposter, of course, her old memories stolen by Administrator. But Kirito had tried to save the lives of Deusolbert and even Fanatio, who had nearly killed him...so perhaps...

"No. That wouldn't happen."

He shook his head, forcing himself to dispel those thoughts. It was pointless to think about it. As long as he could get to the top floor and retrieve the memory fragment stored there and return it to Alice's soul, her entire memory of being a knight would vanish. Then at last, the real Alice, the person he adored more than any other, would return.

When she awakened again, he would hold her tight and at last say, *I'm going to keep you safe...forever.* That moment would come soon, by tomorrow or perhaps even that night.

Now was the time to drive those thoughts away and focus on getting closer.

The bells somewhere in the cathedral tolled seven as he came to the end of the stairs. Eugeo counted each time he arrived at a flat landing; that number was now ten. That made this the ninetieth floor. He was approaching the heart of the Axiom Church's power now.

There was no indication of any staircase continuing upward in the large entrance hall, just a single massive doorway on the north end. It suggested that, like the fiftieth and eightieth floors, the ninetieth would be one wide-open chamber. And within it, more powerful foes than anything he'd seen yet.

Can I really win? All on my own? he wondered, standing at the end of the hall. Fanatio had nearly killed Kirito, and Alice was even more powerful. How would he manage someone notably stronger than them?

Upon reflection, it had been Kirito alone who'd suffered the blows in those fights. All Eugeo did was hide behind him and activate his Perfect Weapon Control. Kirito claimed that was the smart thing to do, considering their respective strengths, but now he was gone, and it was up to Eugeo to do all the fighting himself.

He brushed the Blue Rose Sword at his left, feeling the texture of the hilt and guard. He'd be able to use Perfect Control one more time, but just wildly throwing it around wasn't going to help him capture anyone with his ice vines. He needed to over-power his foe with swordplay alone and create an opportunity to use it.

"...Here goes," he told the sword, then lifted a hand and pushed on the white door.

Instantly, he was greeted with bright light, thick smoke, and a continuous booming rumble. *A sacred arts attack?!* he wondered instantly, moving to leap out of the way...until he noticed that the pale substance billowing out of the doorway was not smoke but steam. It merely moistened his hands and sleeves. Through the swirling vapors, he identified what was happening inside the room.

As expected, this entire floor of the cathedral was dedicated to a single vast chamber, and countless lamps shone from its extremely high ceiling. The floor probably had some fancy name like the Corridor of Ghostly Light or Cloudtop Garden, but there was no way to know. The steam hung low to the ground, blocking Eugeo's view, but the place seemed empty.

Eugeo took a few steps into the hall, trying to discern the steam's source. He heard splashing water, and there was a distant rumble that was probably a large stream.

Just then, a draft of cold air from the door rushed through, pushing the wafting steam aside. There was a marble path about five mels wide farther into the chamber. On either side of the walkway the floor dropped, down a series of steps covered by clear water—and hot water, at that. It was at least a mel deep, too. If this entire chamber was full all the way around, he couldn't even imagine how many lils of water it held.

"What...is...this room...?" He gasped.

The water temperature was too hot to support fish or other animals, and the humidity was too unpleasant for some kind of viewing garden. If anything, it would probably feel good to strip off his clothes and jump into the hot...

"Oh...w-wait a second..."

He knelt at the edge of the pathway and stuck his hand in the water. It was neither too hot nor too lukewarm—exactly the sort of thing that Kirito would describe as "just the right temp."

It was an enormous megabath.

"..."

Eugeo exhaled, still on his knees. Back at his family home in Rulid, the bath was not much bigger than a simple water basin, and since he was the youngest, by the time it was his turn, the water was half-gone. The first time he saw the bathhouse at the academy dorm, he couldn't believe it was possible to heat so much water at once.

But that was nothing compared to this place. You could fit all the students from Swordcraft Academy in here with plenty of room to spare. Though they wouldn't allow the male and female students to bathe at the same time, of course...

Eugeo exhaled again and washed both hands, just because he could, being considerate enough not to bother with his face. He proceeded down the marble walkway toward the ascending staircase, which he expected would be on the other end of the room. Surely they wouldn't attack him in a bath...

But this assumption delayed his recognition of what was ahead. In the center of the Great Bath chamber, the walkway bulged into a circle. And when he approached it, Eugeo at last noticed a shadow lurking in the water ahead and to his right.

"—?!"

He leaped back on instinct, putting a hand on his sword handle. The misty figure was large with short hair, suggesting that it was not a woman. He was submerged up to his shoulders, with all his limbs stretched out.

This pose indicated he was simply bathing, rather than waiting in ambush, but Eugeo couldn't afford to be careless. Given the circumstances, the man was almost certainly an enemy. Perhaps it would be best to strike now, while he had the advantage of terrain.

He was about to slide his sword from its sheath when a deep, rusty voice said, "Sorry, you mind waiting first? Just got back to Centoria, and I've been on my dragon for ages. I'm all stiff."

His manner of speaking was rougher than that of anyone they'd met in the cathedral, which surprised Eugeo. The man had a kind of informal simplicity—he was more reminiscent of a rural farmer than a knight.

Eugeo was frozen, unsure what to do. The water sloshed, parting the clouds of steam hovering over the bath. The owner of the voice had stood up, droplets pouring off his frame. He stood with his back to the intruder, hands on hips, rolling his head around on his neck and groaning. It looked totally careless, but even with his hand on his sword, Eugeo couldn't take a step.

The man was huge. His knees were submerged in the bath, but even then, he was nearly two mels tall. His steely blue-gray hair was shorn short, revealing a shockingly thick neck connected to two very wide shoulders. His biceps were like logs built for swinging even the largest greatswords with ease.

But the most eye-catching detail was his rippling layers of back muscles. Back at school, Eugeo served as page to Golgorosso Balto, who was quite imposing himself, but this man was on another level entirely. He didn't seem young, but the muscle around his midriff was still perfectly taut.

Eugeo was so arrested by the body of this warrior god that he initially failed to notice the countless scars crisscrossing his skin. In fact, they all seemed to be either arrow or blade injuries. Even deep wounds would heal without a trace if treated right away with high-level healing arts, so this spoke to a number of harrowing battles.

This had to be the commander of the Integrity Knights. The strongest one. The greatest obstacle Eugeo would face on his way to the top of the cathedral...

In that case, now was the time to strike, when he had neither weapon nor armor. Kirito would certainly do it.

Eugeo knew what needed to be done, but once again he froze.

He couldn't tell whether the man was exposing his back to him as a sign of carelessness or as an exhibition of total confidence. If anything, it seemed like he was enticing Eugeo to attack.

The man finished stretching, totally unconcerned with the boy, then sloshed north through the water. On the walkway just ahead, there was a basket that most likely contained his clothes. He strode up the step onto the lip of the walkway, removed a pair of underpants from the basket, and put them on. Next he donned a thin top—it appeared to be a kimono from the eastern empire, with a wide sash that matched the fabric.

"Sorry to keep you waiting," he said, facing Eugeo at last. His features were chiseled and bold, in keeping with his deep, manly voice. The crisp wrinkles lining his mouth indicated that he was over forty when he became an Integrity Knight, but his cheekbones and the bridge of his nose were hard and strong. The most distinct feature of all was the powerful eyes under his full brows.

There was no real hostility in the pale-blue irises, but even standing over fifteen mels away, Eugeo felt a powerful pressure from them. It was interest in the foe he would soon overpower that dwelled in those eyes, and eagerness for the battle itself. Only one with absolute confidence in his skill could produce such a look. He was like Kirito in that way.

Once he was done tying his sash, he held out a hand to the basket. A longsword rose up from the bottom and fit into his burly hand. He lifted it to his shoulder and walked barefoot across the marble toward Eugeo.

The man came to a stop just eight mels away, stroked his lightly bearded chin, and said, "Now, can you tell me just one thing before we fight?"

"…What is it?"

"Is, er…the vice commander…is Fanatio…dead?" he asked, in the tone of one inquiring about the dinner menu. Eugeo felt momentarily offended—she was his subordinate, after all. But then he noticed an awkward artifice to the man's expression: He'd glanced off to the side. He truly wanted to know the answer, couldn't wait to find out, but didn't want to seem too obvious about it. That, too, reminded Eugeo of someone very familiar.

"...She's alive. She's being tended to now...I believe," he answered.

The man let out a long breath and said, "That's good. In that case, I won't take your life, either."

"Wha...?"

Eugeo lost his voice again. He felt so inferior that it wasn't even worth trying to call the man's bluff. Kirito had once told him that belief in oneself could be a weapon of its own, but even he hadn't exhibited this much confidence in the presence of an enemy. The enormous man had a wealth of confidence as unshakeable as a boulder thanks to something neither he nor Kirito had: the experience of having won countless furious battles, enough to leave his body covered in their scars.

But while Eugeo might not come close to matching him in victories, he had vanquished more than one Integrity Knight on the way here—the very title this fellow wore. If he felt overwhelmed before they even started fighting, he'd be shaming the knights he defeated, Golgorosso and the other people at the academy who'd helped train him, and most of all, his black-haired partner.

Mustering all the courage he could, Eugeo glared at the man facing him. He tensed his gut to ensure his voice would not falter.

"I don't like it."

"Oh?" the man said amusedly, his hand paused on the inside of his eastern-style clothing. "What don't you like, boy?"

"Fanatio is not your only subordinate. There's Eldrie and the Four Whirling Blades...and Alice as well. Don't you care for their lives or deaths?"

"Oh...that's what you mean," he murmured, looking up and scratching the side of his head with the hilt of his longsword.

"Well…Eldrie is little Alice's disciple, and the other four belong to Fanatio: Dakira, Jace, Hoveren, and Geero. But Fanatio is *my* disciple. I'm not the kind to fight out of hatred and hostility, but if a disciple of mine gets killed, I need to avenge them. That's all."

He smirked, then added, "Actually…little Alice might consider me her teacher…but just between you and me, if we fought, I couldn't say who'd win. When she was an apprentice knight six years ago, sure. But now…"

"Six years ago…apprentice knight…?" Eugeo murmured, forgetting his anger for a moment.

Six years ago was just two years after Alice had been taken from Rulid. The Integrity Knights' names included numbers in the sacred tongue, and according to what Kirito had taught him while they ascended the stairs, Alice was thirty, Eldrie was thirty-one, and Deusolbert was seven. Based on the high value of her number, he doubted that she was converted all that long ago…

"But…Alice is the thirtieth Integrity Knight…isn't she?" he asked.

The man looked briefly confused. "Ohhh. The apprentices aren't given numbers, as a general rule. She was officially made number thirty when she was turned into a proper knight last year. She was certainly powerful enough to be a knight six years ago, but she was so young then…"

"But…Fizel and Linel had numbers, and they were very young."

Hearing those names made the man scowl as if he'd chewed a bitter bug. "Those little squirts had a…different…route into knighthood. They had a special exception that allowed them to receive numbers as apprentices. Did you fight them? I'm surprised you're alive—for a different reason than I'm surprised you beat Fanatio."

"I nearly lost my head, actually. They paralyzed me with Ruberyl's poisoned steel," Eugeo admitted.

The man had known Alice when she was an apprentice knight. Perhaps that meant Alice had undergone the Synthesis Ritual that had covered up her memories six years ago…when she was thirteen. And ever since then, she'd been living here in the cathedral, believing that she'd been summoned from the celestial realm to be an Integrity Knight...

Shrugging, the large man said, "Look, you're not going to get the best of me, and if she's just as tough as I am, I doubt you cut her in two, either. From what the damn prime senator tells me, you've got a partner. If he ain't here, then I presume he must be battling the young lady somewhere."

"...You've got the right idea," Eugeo admitted, gripping his sword hilt. Something in the way the man spoke was dulling Eugeo's hostility, but this was no time to be lax. He narrowed his eyes and taunted, "If I strike you down, who will come out for vengeance next?"

"Heh! Don't worry about that. I've got no teacher." The man grinned, lowering the sword from his shoulder so he could draw it. With his left hand, he thrust the empty sheath into his wide waist sash.

The thick, dark blade was smoothly polished, but the little nicks and imperfections from a plethora of battles over the years glinted in the light from the ceiling. The guard and hilt looked like the same kind of steel as the blade itself, but unlike the legendary weapons of the other Integrity Knights, this one had no ostentatious decoration.

Even from a distance, it was clear this weapon was not to be trifled with. It had tasted the blood of many, many foes over a mind-bending span of time. There was a kind of cursed energy infused into the dull gray metal.

Eugeo exhaled slowly and slid his own sword free. He wasn't using Perfect Control, but the pale-blue sword was exuding a chill that turned the nearby steam into glittering frost, perhaps channeling its owner's nerves.

With a grand movement befitting his size, the man held up his sword nearly vertical with his body and drew his leg back into a firm, poised stance. It was similar to the High-Norkia Lightning Slash but not the same. With his sword perfectly straight up, he'd need extra movement before he initiated the technique. So Eugeo made the stance for the Aincrad style's Sonic Leap.

The mysterious Aincrad style—of which Kirito was the only user, as far as Eugeo knew—had many different secret techniques, all named with the exotic sacred tongue. The sacred tongue was taught to the founder of the Axiom Church when the three goddesses created the world. There were no dictionaries for it in the academy's library—and according to the instructors, none even in the four Imperial Palaces.

Vocabulary words for the sacred arts were the only words one was allowed to know. So Eugeo, as a dutiful student, understood the meaning of just a select few sacred words, like *element* and *generate*.

But Kirito, despite losing all memory before he ran into Eugeo in the woods two years before, seemed to know a variety of unfamiliar sacred words, including ones in his techniques: Sonic Leap meant "jumping at the speed of sound," apparently. Eugeo didn't know how fast sound traveled, but like the name suggested, it did allow him to jump forward about ten mels with astonishing speed. If you unleashed it at the moment the enemy took the first step forward to close the gap, you were practically certain to seize the initiative.

Eugeo let the tension go and held up his sword to rest on his right shoulder. New furrows appeared in the man's brow.

"I don't recognize that stance, boy. Do you use the continuous blade?" he mumbled.

"…!"

Eugeo sucked in a breath. Technically, his Sonic Leap skill was a singular technique. But in the sense that it wasn't taught in any other school in the human lands, it was just like the Aincrad style's signature feature: combination techniques. This man's instinct and experience were evident from his starting stance alone.

But just because he could sense that Eugeo wielded a continuous style did not mean he could predict the Aincrad school's specific teachings—not unless he had fought Kirito before his memory loss.

"...And what if I do use combination skills?" he rasped.

The man snorted. "No, there was a knight in the Dark Territory who could use it. We had a number of fights, and I don't remember them fondly...You see, I'm not the type to use tricky, fussy swings like that."

"...So you'd prefer me to use an orthodox style?"

"No, no. Use whatever you like. I'm just letting you know that I'll be jumping straight to my best," he said, mouth curling into a grin. He thrust his upright sword even higher.

An instant later, Eugeo held his breath again; the worn gray metal rippled like heat haze. At first he thought it was steam from the bath, but the more he watched, the more he was convinced the sword itself had lost its firmness.

Maybe the sword is already under Perfect Control.

Eugeo's mind raced as he held his attack pose. It wasn't long ago that the mysterious Cardinal had taught him how to use Perfect Weapon Control, but after using it in battle a few times, Eugeo was starting to understand the ability better.

It was similar to sword techniques in the way it gave the weapon power, but Perfect Control was sacred arts through and through and required an incantation. Like your typical sacred arts, one could perform the base command and have it on hold for a time before it was activated with the code *Enhance Armament.*

The actual amount of holding time depended on the caster's potential and training. If Eugeo kept quiet and focused hard, he could last for several minutes, but Kirito, who had phenomenal concentration when it mattered most, could do so and hold a conversation.

Eugeo didn't yet know what form this man's Perfect Control took, but it was obvious since he'd been talking at length that this man was extremely skilled with it. For his part, Eugeo didn't have time to start chanting the words, and his ice roses weren't going to be very effective in a steamy bathhouse.

That left one option: use Sonic Leap in the instant the man used his own technique or Perfect Control arts, in the hope of clinching the fight. He would be expecting Eugeo to use a combination attack, and hopefully he would be taken by surprise when it was an ultra-speed jump.

He tensed his gut, focused all his concentration forward, and watched.

The distance between them was about eight mels.

Neither Norkia style nor its advanced counterpart, High-Norkia style, had a technique that could cover that much ground at once. So if the man swung his sword from his position without stepping closer, that "best" attack of his would be some kind of Perfect Weapon Control that extended the reach of his swings. Eugeo would have to evade it somehow and strike with a counter.

As expected, the man stood in place and slowly swung his upright sword downward. The smile was gone from his lips, which opened to bellow, "Taste the blade of Integrity Knight Commander Bercouli Synthesis One!!"

For just an instant, Eugeo wondered, *Where have I heard that before?* But he hastily overrode his side thoughts to focus only on the enemy's movement.

The so-called commander's left foot pounded heavily onto the marble stone. All the steam in his vicinity shredded into nothing.

Incredibly fast and yet somehow graceful, his powerful hips, chest, shoulders, and arms rotated. First his sword tilted to the right, then it swiped out directly level. Eugeo could sense that this was the greatest of swordplay taught by the orthodox schools. The movement was simple and unadorned yet utterly polished through years and years of experience.

But all the orthodox schools of swordfighting had a weakness in common. Because their forms were so proud and distinct, it was easy to predict the attack's trajectory. By the time the commander's sword was slicing flat through the white steam, Eugeo was already in the air, jumping forward to his left. He would be able to dodge cleanly, even if the sword exhibited some kind of Perfect Control attack.

The air rippled at his right ear, but he felt no pain or impact.

I dodged it! he thought, then landed and activated Sonic Leap.

"Rrraaaah!"

His sword took on a green glow tinged with yellow. An invisible power accelerated his body, turning Eugeo into a gust of wind that burst toward the knights' commander, who had just finished his own swing.

Behind him, the burst from the sword he had just dodged continued until it hit the doors of the bath with a huge—

Nothing.

No sound. Not even a vibration.

Had the slash from the commander been that slow? Or had it dissipated before it reached the doors?

That couldn't be. That would mean this man, who should be stronger than Deusolbert and Fanatio, had a Perfect Weapon Control with a weaker range than Eldrie, who'd been an Integrity Knight for only a month. Eldrie's Frostscale Whip struck dozens of mels away like lightning.

It couldn't be true. So was the commander's attack not one of an elongated attack range? In fact, Eugeo didn't get hit at all. That meant all the man did was a simple swing. An ordinary exhibition of a form, the same thing that every student at Swordcraft Academy did during a test.

Is he toying with me? Or does he think a mere student will turn tail and retreat from a single free swing?

The thought burned in his mind—and delayed his realization.

There was something right between the path of Eugeo's rampaging attack and the stationary man. A horizontal, transparent ripple suspended in the air. Just like the heat haze that surrounded the man's sword before he swung it.

And that's...right where he swung his sword...

A deep chill ran down his back. Instinctually he tried to cancel his charge, but once initiated, a technique couldn't be stopped that easily. He tugged on his sword and scraped his foot on the floor, but the best he managed was a slight dip in speed.

Then Eugeo's body passed through the floating haze. A burst of blazing heat passed through him from left pectoral to right flank. He was rocketed through the air like a scrap of cloth caught in a gale, rotating madly. Blood gushed from the massive gash on his chest, tracing a spiral through the air.

He landed flat on his back in the bath on the left side of the walkway. A plume of water shot up, and soon the water around the impact was a vivid red.

"Grg...aaah...!"

He spat up the hot water that flooded his mouth; there was red spittle there, too. The gash had reached his lungs, then. If he hadn't slowed his momentum that little bit before he hit the haze, it might have completely severed his torso.

"System...Call. Generate...Luminous Element...," he said, casting a healing art as he floated. Fortunately, there was plenty of warm water around, which had much more sacred power than when cold. But Eugeo wasn't a skilled enough caster to heal such a deep wound in a short amount of time.

He stopped the blood loss, though, and got unsteadily to his feet. The knights' commander stared down at him from the walkway. The sword was already back in its sheath, and his right hand was thrust into the opening of his kimono, resting there.

"That was a bit dangerous, there. Didn't expect you to come rushing up so fast. Sorry, nearly ended up killing you."

His words seemed really informal for such a dire situation, but Eugeo didn't have time to argue over that. Through pained lungs, he rasped, "Wh...what was...that...you did...?"

"I warned you I'd be giving you my best. And I didn't just swing and slice through the air. You might say...I sliced the future, just a moment ahead."

It took some time for the commander's words to make concrete sense to Eugeo. The throbbing of his wound, which felt like ice in the midst of so much hot water, impeded his thoughts.

Sliced…the future?

It seemed to match the phenomenon he'd witnessed. Eugeo activated Sonic Leap after the swordsman had already swung his blade. But the instant he touched the path where it had been, he suffered a terrible wound, as though the sword had struck him in that passing moment.

But that wasn't exactly right. If anything, it was like the force of the slice had somehow remained, hanging in the air. He'd seen the wavering ripple right up to the moment his body made contact with it.

In order to land a successful hit with a sword, you had to cut the right place at the right time. If either of the two weren't accurate, the sword would not strike true. Most likely, the knights' commander's Perfect Weapon Control gave him expanded control over the latter. Even after swinging, the force of his sword stayed in place. In other words, it cut the enemy who would fill that space in the future.

Visually, it was the least impressive of all the times he'd seen Perfect Control, but it was perhaps the most fearsome. Every space the enemy's sword passed through turned into a deadly trap. And the length of its effectiveness was much longer than a combination technique, which was itself a method of increasing an attack's time. There was no way he could force a close melee battle.

A long-distance fight, then.

The commander's Perfect Control enabled him to extend his attack time but not the range of his swing. Meanwhile, the range of Eugeo's ice vines was over thirty mels. The real question was whether the Blue Rose Sword could use its ability properly in a place with so much hot water. At the very least, he'd have to count on a delay between activation and taking effect. In other words, Eugeo would need to lure the enemy close enough to use his sword's vine ability and still have it work whether or not the man caught on to it.

It would be difficult, but he had no other choice.

Eugeo traced his chest with his left hand. The flesh stung, but the healing was firm enough that he could move about without reopening the wound. He wasn't fully healed by a long shot—he'd probably lost a third of his life—but he could stand, and he could swing.

"System Call," he said quietly, letting his voice hide under the thunder of the pipes gushing water into the bath from each corner of the room. He didn't expect the commander would let him get away with the chant, but if anything, the way the man leisurely crossed his arms and chatted made it seem like he was intentionally giving Eugeo time.

"The first time I saw a knight of darkness use a continuous blade, it was just after I'd been made an Integrity Knight. At first I got beat, and beat good. But I escaped with my life, and I racked this dumb old brain of mine to find the reason I lost."

He rubbed a scar on his chin, likely a memento of that experience.

"But once I figured it out, it turned out not to be that tricky. Basically, the swordsmanship I'd learned was all about putting as much power into a single swing as possible, while the continuous blade was all about deflecting the enemy attack and hitting him with your own. It ain't a question about which of the two is more practical in a fight. Doesn't matter how hard you swing if you miss the mark. The best you can do is give them a refreshing breeze…"

His lips twisted into a grimace, and he let loose a puff of air.

"But I wasn't clever enough to begin learning the continuous blade right away, just because I'd figured out its point. If the pontifex really wanted an Integrity Knight, she could've summoned one a bit less stubborn."

Eugeo felt his curiosity grow, even as his mind was occupied with chanting his sacred art. The self-proclaimed commander of the Integrity Knights himself had lost his prior memories, just like the others. But even if he, too, forgot his story, was it possible that the rest of the world would simply fail to remember the wielder of such an overpowering sword? Ever since Eugeo had heard him announce himself earlier, something had been steadily eating away at him.

Bercouli Synthesis One. That's what he had called himself.

He knew he'd heard that name before. It was either a previous champion of the Four-Empire Unification Tournament or some general of the Imperial Knights.

But the man paid little heed to Eugeo's piercing gaze or the muttered incantation under his breath.

"So I racked my brain for a way to help my sword hit the enemy better. And the answer I landed on was this." He slid the simple steel sword out of its sheath. "This sword was originally part of a Divine Object stuck to the wall of Central Cathedral, a thing called a *clock*. In its place is now a Bell of Time-Tolling that measures the hour, but in the past, it was a big circle of numbers with a huge needle that pointed to them. Apparently it was around at the world's very creation. The pontifex had a weird, unfamiliar name for it...called it a System Clock, as I recall."

Eugeo didn't recognize the sacred words. But neither did he know the common-tongue *clock* Bercouli mentioned. The man had a distant gaze in his eyes, as if staring into the long-lost past.

"As the pontifex says, 'The clock does not indicate time—it creates time.' I had no idea what she meant by it, though. But this blade is what resulted when the hand of that clock was reforged. Little Alice's Osmanthus Blade cuts through the horizontal axis of space, while this one cuts the vertical axis of time. It's called the Time-Splitting Sword."

Eugeo found it difficult to envision this clock's form, but he felt like he understood what the knights' commander was saying. The power from the sword's swing could pierce through time and hold its place. With that ability, there was no need at all to chain multiple slashes together, like the Aincrad style. And the only reason that a combination attack needed to be combined was to lengthen the time of the attack without having to recover and refocus. If Bercouli's sword had both the power of a singular attack and the striking accuracy of a combination, it was basically invincible—as long as you were within its range.

As Bercouli himself had said so poetically, there was only one way to counteract it: fight not with time but with the expanse of space.

But no sooner had the thought occurred to Eugeo than the knight grinned. "And now you think you must attack from a distance. They all do after they see my technique."

Eugeo felt a twinge of panic at being read so easily, but there was no stopping the chant now. He might be able to predict that Eugeo would attempt a long-range attack, but he wouldn't know what kind of attack.

Whether aware of Eugeo's internal logic or not, the commander shrugged and said, "The fact that all the Integrity Knights who were summoned after me, including Fanatio and Alice, have a tendency to choose long-range Perfect Control, probably has something to do with seeing what I can do...I suspect. They're all very stubborn in that way, you see. But let me be clear that I've never lost a sparring match with any of them. I told them that if they ever beat me, I'll make them the commander on the spot. One day, little Alice might find a way to beat me. In short, I'm looking forward to this. I want to see what your sword can do, if it really did knock them out left and right."

"...You sound very confident."

Eugeo had finished chanting the bulk of his sacred arts a few seconds earlier. But something about the intense concentration coupled with his nerves allowed him to murmur the statement without losing the stocked magic.

So Bercouli was admitting that his long speech was meant to give Eugeo time to exhibit his most powerful ability. He knew that whatever it was, he could overcome it the first time he saw it.

And frustrating as it was to admit, even if he could capture Bercouli with the vines of ice roses, Eugeo had zero confidence that he could deplete the man's life. It was a technique designed to stop movement, after all. And that surely wouldn't be entirely effective against him, either. At best, it might stop him cold for a couple of seconds. How he used that brief moment would determine the battle's outcome.

Eugeo rose from the bath, water cascading from his body. Just rising the three steps to the marble walkway caused the wound on his chest to throb painfully. He wouldn't have the strength to heal the next attack.

"Heh! Come for me, boy. And let me warn you: I won't go easy on the next one."

He squeezed the hilt of the Time-Splitting Sword tucked into the sash of his kimono and chuckled. On the walkway twenty mels away, Eugeo brandished the Blue Rose Sword in front of him. With the art on standby, the blade was already coated in thin frost, dusting the hovering steam nearby with ice.

Kirito would have a snappy comeback in a situation like this, but Eugeo's mouth was parched and stiff, unable to work smoothly. He took a deep breath and carefully spoke the activation words for Perfect Weapon Control.

"Enhance…Armament."

A chilly wind swirled up from his feet and burst in all directions. He flipped his sword around to hold it in reverse and slammed it right into the stone floor. Instantly, the water on the smooth marble froze into a mirror surface. With a sound like a tree splitting apart, the band of ice raced toward Bercouli.

The walkway was five mels across, but the width of the Blue Rose Sword's ice wave was nearly ten. The water's surface on either side of the stone developed an icy film, but its spread was weaker and slower, due to the water's heat. Still, no excuses were possible at this desperate juncture.

Focusing all thoughts into his right hand, Eugeo clenched the sword ever tighter. He roared, and the frosted floor sprouted not vines but sharp thorns. They formed a thick pillar of ice that rippled down the walkway toward Bercouli, vicious glinting spikes covering the entire floor. But the commander merely tightened at the mouth and stayed put, standing in a slight crouch. He had no intention of escaping into the water.

Seeing his opponent stand firm like a fortress, Eugeo realized what he had to do. If he didn't risk everything in this fight, he would never win.

He pulled the Blue Rose Sword from the floor and raced after the carpet of ice. His moment of opportunity would arise when the dozens of ice spears reached Bercouli.

Naturally, the commander could see Eugeo charging toward him, but he didn't show the tiniest smidgen of reaction. He simply spread his feet and willed power into the sword at his left side.

"Hrrng!!"

He bellowed and swung. The carpet of ice spears wasn't yet within range, so the powerful slice cut only empty air—but the Time-Splitting Sword could sever the future.

Craaash!!

Half a second later, the plethora of ice stalagmites burst. Not one made it past the slice that Bercouli placed in front of them. With almost detestable confidence, the commander returned his blade to an upright position to prepare for Eugeo's follow-up.

But Eugeo had the enemy in his sights now and held his weapon high overhead. The tiny shards of ice floating around it caught the light from the ceiling, fogging his vision, but it affected his foe equally.

"Seyaaa!!"

"Roahh!!"

They roared together. Eugeo's sword traced a pale-blue line in the air, while Bercouli's met his with a gray trail behind it.

The next moment, Eugeo's sword shattered with a thin, tinkling scream.

Bercouli's eyes widened just a bit, probably because he was taken aback by the lack of resistance. Eugeo hardly felt a thing, either.

But he knew that was coming. Right before his charge, Eugeo had tossed aside the Blue Rose Sword and broken off an icicle to use as a weapon.

Bercouli had swung to deflect Eugeo's weapon. If the sword had been proper steel instead of ice, the impact would have knocked him back on his heels. But because the ice simply gave way without resisting, it allowed Eugeo to keep speeding forward, past Bercouli's defenses.

"Yaaaah!"

He turned his body and rammed his left shoulder into the commander's stomach. This was an unarmed attack of the Aincrad style called Meteor Break—it supposedly referred to a rock from the sky that breaks through anything in its way. It didn't technically activate, because he wasn't holding his sword, but when combined with the man's unexpected overswing, it succeeded in knocking the large man off balance, disrupting his center of gravity.

Normally Eugeo would continue with a level swipe on the right. But instead, the boy spread his arms and grappled around the commander's waist.

"Nwah…"

This impromptu push knocked the hefty fellow back, loosening his upper half. This would be the first and last opportunity.

"*Yaaaah!!*" Eugeo bellowed, disguising the pain of his wound as a masculine roar, and hurled the commander and himself with all his strength toward the bath on the right. Bercouli tensed with his left leg in an attempt to resist, but his bare sole slipped on the icy stone. After he was airborne, the sting of landing in water punched his chest.

But that sensation was nothing compared to the blinding, all-enveloping chill.

"What the…?!" Bercouli exclaimed yet again, with Eugeo clinging to his waist. The bathwater had been scalding just minutes ago, and now it was nearly freezing. No wonder he was shocked.

Eugeo held down the man with his left hand and used his right to search around on the floor of the bath. *It should be just around here…*

Half by meticulous design, half by luck, his fingers grazed the familiar hilt of his sword.

Soon after, Bercouli threw Eugeo off him by brute force and started to rise, but not before Eugeo thrust the Blue Rose Sword into the base of the bath and commanded, "Freeeeeze!!"

This was the battle's crucial juncture.

The Blue Rose Sword froze only a small percentage of the vast bath. There was still plenty of hot water around it. In order to freeze it all, you'd need ten sacred arts casters generating ice elements for most of an hour. But there was no other choice here.

Perfect Weapon Control unleashed the memory of the sword, bringing forth power that would be impossible otherwise. It was the wise, mysterious Cardinal who'd said that. She'd made Eugeo and Kirito travel the path of their swords' memories to put together the Perfect Control arts for each.

Eugeo's Blue Rose Sword was a Divine Object that originally came from the chunk of ice that sat at the very top of the End Mountains' tallest peak in the north. It was cold there even in the middle of summer, and because the ice failed to melt all year long, it kept all creatures away. For decades and decades, that eternal ice passed a solitary existence.

One spring, there was a breeze that carried over the mountains and dropped a tiny seed right near the eternal ice. Day by day, the ice let a bit of itself melt, providing a small amount of water to The Seed. Eventually, it found root and budded despite the freezing cold, and when summer arrived, it bloomed a small but beautiful flower. It was a rose, even bluer than the northern skies.

Delighted to have a friend at last, the eternal ice spoke to the flower at every opportunity. But one day, as autumn was coming to a close, the flower said, "I won't be able to survive the cold of winter. We'll be parting soon."

The ice lamented. It cried and cried at the loss of its only friend, which shrank its body. The flower said, "Before I shrivel up and wither away, will you lock me inside you? That way, even after I die, my body will remain forever."

The eternal ice granted the blue rose's wish. From its own tears, it carefully formed a pool of water around the blue rose and prayed, *Freeze, freeze, freeze forever.* The prayer was so strong, it even froze the ice's own heart.

When the blue rose froze within the ice, the frozen ice no longer spoke or thought for itself. It had shed so many tears that the only thing left on the mountaintop was a piece of ice that had elongated into the shape of a sword, with a single blue rose trapped inside.

It could have all just been a dream that Eugeo had inside that enormous library. He had no idea how that rough ice approximation of a sword had turned into a real weapon and moved from the peak down to the cave underneath, where the white dragon hoarded it. And of course, it was impossible that a chunk of ice and a rose could have minds and feelings.

And yet, if it was supposed to be just a dream, how could he still tangibly feel that prayer from the hunk of ice inside him? The wish for all the sadness, the pain, the life, even time itself to freeze forever...

Give me your strength, Blue Rose Sword! he prayed, letting loose a shout.

"Release...Recollection!!"

This was the second stage of Perfect Weapon Control: the command for Memory Release, fully unlocking the weapon's hidden power. Cardinal had said they weren't advanced enough to use it yet, but maybe now he could—and if not now, then when?

In his hand, the sword shook.

Then there was the stunning sound of countless panes of glass shattering all at once throughout the bathhouse. A ring of bright-blue light spread quickly out of Eugeo's hand. All the water it touched froze so fast, even the ripples were preserved.

In mere seconds, the enormous bath was frozen white. The terrific, incapacitating chill forced a moan from Eugeo's lips. You would never feel a temperature that cold, even standing naked in the Rulid forest in midwinter. If he closed his eyes, he wouldn't be able to tell whether it was ice on his skin, or burning iron.

He wanted to brush off the frost whitening his eyelashes, but his left hand was under the water, holding Bercouli down, while his right had the Blue Rose Sword in a reverse grip near the bottom. Only blinking rapidly could knock the crystals off, giving him a view of his foe through the thick mist.

Bercouli the Integrity Knight Commander was stuck in the ice up to his neck. Because he'd been trying to push himself up, both his left hand and his sword-holding right were near the bottom of the bath. Like Eugeo, he was immobilized.

The commander grumbled, tiny icicles crumbling from his brows and beard. "Never thought I'd see a swordsman who throws his sword away in the face of the enemy…Is this a tactic of your own devising?"

"…No," Eugeo struggled to say through numb lips. "My partner taught it to me. He said that anything on the battlefield can be used as a weapon or a trap." Bercouli closed his eyes and appeared to think about this, then broke into a grin. More bits of ice sprinkled off his lips.

"Hmph. I see. Making use of the lay of the land…Well, I'll admit that you got one over on me, but I'm afraid I can't just concede defeat to you." He sucked in a breath and held it.

Eugeo was nervous, wondering what he intended to do. If the man started chanting a sacred art, he'd have to prepare a counteracting art instantly.

Bercouli's pale-blue eyes opened. His lips parted to reveal bared animal fangs that emitted a splitting cry.

"Nrrrng!!"

Several thick veins rose on his forehead. Cords of muscle bunched on the parts of his neck visible above the ice, turning his skin bright red.

"Wha…?" Eugeo gasped. Bercouli was trying to break through the thick ice using nothing but sheer muscle power.

It was impossible. Even with full movement and plenty of space, you'd have a terrible time attempting to break a block of ice this thick with your bare hands. And he was trying to do it while completely immobilized from the neck down.

His clenched white teeth creaked with a sound like metal scraping. Those blue eyes burned like they were going to emit their own light. Even the subzero air surrounding him could not stop an even colder sensation from running down Eugeo's spine.

Then there was a small but undeniable crack.

A fracture line ran through the ice between them. It cracked and split into two. And then another. Once again, Eugeo realized this man was an extraordinary, superhuman specimen. The Integrity Knights were chosen from among the handful of the very best warriors in all the empires, and this man stood above them all. He was the most powerful fighter in the world. A living legend who had spent a century or two in battle.

Not a single instant of carelessness could happen against such an opponent. Of course, Eugeo hadn't expected that freezing both himself and the enemy would be the end of the battle. His true intention was yet to come: a forced battle of attrition as their life values sank.

Deep under the surface of the ice, Eugeo gripped the hilt of his sword, which was still in its Memory Release state, and focused his thoughts. If the memories he saw were true, then the Blue Rose Sword had a slightly different genesis than Kirito's black sword, Bercouli's Time-Splitting Sword, and Fanatio's Heaven-Splitting Sword. Unlike theirs, his had two distinct entities for its source: the eternal ice and the rose locked inside it.

The ice's power was to freeze all things. And the rose's power... was to cause life to flower.

"Bloom, blue roses!!" he screamed, and countless buds dotted the surface of the ice. They rotated as they grew, extending clear blue petals as thin as razors. Each rose bloomed with the chime of a bell, until there were hundreds and hundreds of flowers. It was a sight astonishingly beautiful and unfathomably harsh—all the flowers were growing and blooming through the consumption of Eugeo's and Bercouli's lives.

He felt his limbs growing numb, his vision dimming. Not only could he not feel the chill; he couldn't even sense the hardness of the ice pressing against his skin. Sheer numbing lack of sensation covered his entire body.

Bercouli's reddened skin was turning paler, too; trying to break through the ice was sapping all his strength. For the first time in the fight, his proud features no longer looked totally confident.

"Kid...were you planning on taking us both down...from the start?"

"Don't get...the wrong idea," Eugeo rasped, struggling to lift his heavy lids. "The only area where I might have an advantage... is the amount...of life. Fanatio suffered the same wound as my partner and collapsed at the same moment...which would mean that Integrity Knights still have the same amount of life as regular people...isn't that right?"

While he spoke, brilliant points of light began floating up from the hundreds of icy roses. The thundering sound of the main faucets providing the bath with water was gone now, a sign that the ice had reached even them.

Both Bercouli and Eugeo were covered with so much ice, only their faces were exposed. If he could see their Stacia Windows, they would indicate that their life was dropping at an alarming rate. Eugeo desperately fought back against his sudden desire to sleep, keeping his mouth working.

"Based on your looks...I assume you became a knight after you turned forty...and that means your maximum life value is lowered. But my life is close to its peak...Even after taking that blow, my number should still be higher. That was my bet."

No sooner were the words out of Eugeo's mouth than Bercouli's eyes shot open. His face contorted, breaking the icicles hanging from his forehead and nose. "What the hell...did you just say?"

It would have been difficult just to stay conscious, but there was a burning fire raging in the commander's eyes. "When I *became* a knight...? You're acting like you know what our previous lives were like."

Eugeo blinked, gathering all his remaining strength to reply, "I cannot...forgive...that part of you people."

The sudden surge of emotion from his gut caused him to briefly lose feeling all over his body. "You forget who and what you are... you know nothing of the true form of the Axiom Church you serve...and you pretend that you're the good guys, the only real protectors of the law. You're not knights who were summoned from Heaven by the pontifex. You were born from a mother who gave you the name Bercouli. You're a human being, just like me!" he screamed.

And just then, in that moment, Eugeo realized *who* the mighty man was.

The shock was so sudden, a gasp escaped his lips. Bercouli... the name of the man in the old stories his grandfather told him. He founded Rulid Village three *hundred* years ago and served as its first chief man-at-arms. He went spelunking in the cave under the End Mountains, where he snuck up on the sleeping white dragon in search of a fabled sword...the Blue Rose Sword, which was now in Eugeo's right hand.

For a moment, he wondered if this was some descendent who shared Bercouli's name, but then Eugeo abandoned that idea. When the Integrity Knights' life was prevented from charting its natural decline, aging became impossible. Here he was, in the flesh. The hero Eugeo had admired as a child...and the protagonist of "Bercouli and the Northern White Dragon," the fairy tale he hadn't thought of since that summer Alice was taken away. Only now, the man had no memory of his life at the founding of Rulid.

Somehow, Eugeo recovered from his brief but monumental shock. "B...Bercouli. You...you should recognize...my sword."

A few inches below the surface of the ice, the Blue Rose Sword was still glowing, expelling its full chilling force. The knights' commander and hero of a three-hundred-year-old legend glanced down under the ice. His firm jaw bulged, and air hissed through his clenched teeth. Eugeo was surprised at his eventual answer:

"...I think...I have...seen it...before..."

He closed his eyes slowly, then opened them again.

"When I killed the northern protector...there was a similar sword...in its lair..."

Stunned, Eugeo nearly forgot all about the all-consuming cold that surrounded him. "When you...killed it...?"

An image flashed into his head of exploring the northern cave with Alice, eight years ago. There was a collection of enormous bones inside the central chamber of the cave. They were criss-crossed with fierce gashes—cuts not from some wild animal's fangs or claws but from a metal tool swung by human hands.

"Those dragon bones...*You* did that...? You killed the dragon... from the story...?"

Despite the ice encompassing him, a burning ball of emotion rose in his throat. Eugeo shook his head, feeling something seeping out of his eyes. "Did you really forget everything...? Bercouli, back in the village where I was born, everyone from the elderly to little children knows you as a hero. You were our ancestor, the man who traveled a long way from the big city to found a village in a distant, barren land. The pontifex abducted you, covered up your memories, and made you into the first Integrity Knight. And not just you—Fanatio, Eldrie, Alice...everyone. Before they were made Integrity Knights, they were all...human, just like me."

"Covered up...my memories...?"

Bercouli's gaze had been steady and firm all through the fight, but now it was uncertain, focused on some undefined point in the distance. In a voice just barely audible, he mumbled, "I can't...just take what you said...at face value. But...I'll admit, I've been...skeptical...for a long time...that I was some holy knight brought here from Heaven..."

Bercouli's muscles were relaxed again, no longer clenched. The frost was covering his manly features once more. The tears on Eugeo's cheeks froze, too, disappearing into the film of ice covering his face.

The knowledge that the hero from "Bercouli and the Northern White Dragon" had actually slain the other central figure of the tale filled Eugeo with a sense of helpless loss. The pontifex's power was well beyond his imagining, if even the greatest of warriors could be manipulated and turned into a faithful knight. Perhaps there was no way that a mere pair of student swordsmen could do anything about Administrator...and the Axiom Church.

In the back of his mind, Eugeo could feel his life steadily being sucked away by the blue roses. It would be the same for Bercouli. Through the foggy frost, his gray-blue eyes were half-closed, and he was barely conscious.

So we're both going down...

The realization set off a tiny spark of determination in his heart, a refusal to give up now. But he couldn't even move a finger. Under the ice, he could sense his grip on the Blue Rose Sword dying...

"Hoh-hohhh! Why, what a marvelous sight," a sharp voice said, as unpleasant as fork tines scraping on a metal plate.

Through clouded eyes, Eugeo watched an odd silhouette wobbling closer along the walkway toward them. It was a person, it seemed, but extremely round. It was like someone had attached comically tiny limbs to a giant ball-shaped torso. There was no neck whatsoever, just a similarly round head that grew straight out of the shoulder area. It looked like a child's winter snowman.

But this man's clothes were eye-scorchingly bright. His right half was bright red, while his left half was blue, with golden buttons to hold in his rotund belly. The fellow's trousers were also split colored, as were his shoes.

There wasn't a single hair on his round head, only an angled golden hat resting on the smooth scalp. It was similar in shape to Cardinal's, back in the Great Library, but without the tastefulness. On top of all this, his height was barely over one mel.

Eugeo recalled the midsummer solstice festival in the sixth district of Centoria, where a band of traveling acrobats featured a ball-riding clown dressed in similar attire. But it was clear from the look on the man's face that he was not meant to bring joy and laughter.

His age was impossible to guess. The man's skin was abnormally white, his nose round, and his cheeks sagging. His vivid red lips were wide open in a leering grin. His eyes were very thin, almost crescent shaped, and turned up so that he appeared to be laughing, but the look in his eyes themselves was cold.

The red-and-blue clown hopped along down the walkway, then leaped forcefully onto the frozen bath. His menacingly pointed shoes crunched two of the delicate ice roses.

"Hoh-hohhh! Hoh-hoh-hoh!" he chuckled, though it wasn't clear what he found amusing. The little man clapped his hands and continued reducing the nearby roses to shards of glass. He proceeded toward Eugeo and Bercouli, crunching loudly all the while.

He came to a stop a few mels away, kicked one final rose for good measure, then looked at them at last. His red lips split open, emitting that hideous voice.

"Oh-ho…very poor form, very poor form indeed, Commander. You aren't planning to kick the bucket here, are you? That would be clear rebellion against our lovely pontifex, wouldn't it? If she should awaken, she will be quite furious."

Despite seeming completely unconscious just seconds before, Bercouli opened his trembling mouth to emit a low rasp. "Prime Senator…Chudelkin…You have no reason to interfere in a battle between swordsmen…you cretin…"

"Hoh-hoh-hohhh!" the little clown chuckled, clapping his hands and hopping in place. "Swordsmen! Battle! Oh, how you make me laugh, hoh-hoh-hoh!"

He hissed with laughter in a way no human being ever did.

"Bold words, coming from the man who went as soft as a cloud against this filthy traitor! You didn't use the *flip side* of your Time-Splitting Sword, did you, Commander? You could have killed that arrogant upstart before he so much as uttered a word, if you wanted! And that in itself is treachery to our great lady!!"

"Shut up...I fought...to the utmost of my ability...And more importantly, you lied to me...This kid...ain't some assassin from the Dark Territory...He's far more admirable than a disgusting meat blob like you..."

"Siiiilence! I will wrench your head from your body!!" screeched the little man. His eyes bulged, and he bounced into the air like a ball, then landed feetfirst on Bercouli's head. Then he wobbled back and forth on his perch, screeching and carrying on.

"The only reason we're having this problem in the first place is because you accursed knights can't be trusted to do a single job right! You've been beaten soundly by a pair of miserable children, and I'm afraid the laughter is threatening to split the skin off my sides! When my lady awakens, we'll revisit every single one of the knights...and at the very least, you and the vice commander will be reprocessed, I can tell you that much!"

"What...the hell...are you talking...about...?"

"Oh, enough from you. Shut up, shut up. Just go to sleep."

The little man perched atop Bercouli's head thrust out the pinkie finger of his right hand in a theatrical gesture. Then he licked his red lips and screeched, "System Caaaaall! Deep Freeeeze! Integrator Unit, ID Zero Zero One!"

The sacred art was totally unfamiliar. It was a very short cast, and that meant it wouldn't be super-powerful, if it was an attack. And yet...

"Hrng," grunted Bercouli. Then his body—hair, skin, even clothing—began to turn a dark gray. It wasn't a freezing effect as much as it was turning him into a stone statue. The light went out of his eyes, and his body beneath the ice turned the color of mud. At last, the odd little clown, Prime Senator Chudelkin, hopped off Commander Bercouli's head.

"Hoh-hoh-hee, hoh-hee-hee...As a matter of fact, we've no use for a geezer like you anymore, Number One. We've got a much more useful pawn now...haven't we?"

Then the clown's needle-thin pupils fixed on Eugeo. A horrible fear colder than any ice raced up his spine.

That was when Eugeo hit his limit. He tried to focus on the red-and-blue shoes crunching roses as they approached, but even that was gradually covered in gauzy darkness.

Kirito.

...Alice...

Their names were the last thoughts Eugeo had before he blacked out.

CHAPTER ELEVEN

THE SENATE'S SECRET, MAY 380 HE

1

A violent shiver overtook my body, and my eyes snapped open.

I'd merely closed my lids with my back leaning against the wall, and somehow I'd fallen right to sleep. It was like one of those nightmares where you forget all about it as soon as you awaken. Its only remainder was traces of fear and panic.

I sat up and looked around; nothing seemed different. We were on the narrow terrace ledge running around Central Cathedral at about the eightieth floor. The sun had gone over the horizon long ago, leaving the sky as dark as freshly ground ink. But no matter where I looked, the only light I found coming through the cloud layer was stars, no moon. I felt like I'd heard the eight o'clock bell a while ago, but it would still be some time before the moon goddess blessed us with her meager resources.

The Integrity Knight Alice, as a sign of caution toward me, was kneeling so far away that she was nearly in the reaction range of the nearest gargoyle—er, *minion*—with her eyes closed. I wanted to use this downtime to speak with her and hopefully find a clue that would allow us to avoid hostilities, but she was clearly not interested in chitchat. If only Eugeo were here, he could've used his dagger from Cardinal to prick Alice and solve the issue immediately.

And what was he doing now...?

Now that I thought about it, in the two years since I'd met him near Rulid, there had never been a situation in which I couldn't see him immediately if I wanted—until right now. We slept outdoors on our long journey to Centoria, complained about sharing a cramped inn floor, and even shared dorm rooms the entire time we were at Swordcraft Academy. It was simply a given that we were always together, and although I didn't always think about him, I felt oddly lonely now that we were apart.

No—it wasn't that simple.

Here in the Underworld, the ultimate virtual realm, I'd finally found the very first person of my gender that I could truly call a best friend. It was a bit embarrassing to admit, but that was the plain truth of it.

Before I'd been trapped in the deadly game of *SAO*, I considered all the other boys at school to be childish. I was reserved in my interactions with them. That standoffish nature of mine didn't change much once I was trapped in that virtual floating castle. I'd met men like Klein and Agil who were good, well-adjusted souls that I found common ground with, but we never reached that level of true friendship when you bare your secrets to the other. Even with Asuna, the deepest relationship I'd ever had, I wasn't able to confess my inner weakness until just before the moment Aincrad crumbled and our minds were about to vanish.

I didn't think I had some kind of special power or ability that nobody else did. Between athletics and scholastics, I didn't stand out in any particular area at school.

But when I became a prisoner of *SAO*, I was immediately ranked among the top players of the game pushing our progress forward, a pleasure that I believe bewitched me. And yet, the qualities that helped me stand out were the sum experience of totally immersing myself in full-dive games from the moment they first appeared, and the specific *SAO* knowledge I stockpiled as a beta tester prior to release. None of it had to do with my innate talent or ability as a person.

After I gained my freedom from *SAO*, my reputation for

strength in VR had to be continually upheld, lest I lose that valuable image. I was trapped by the knowledge that others knew me not as the weak, mortal Kazuto Kirigaya, but as Kirito the hero, champion of the game of death. And I couldn't deny that I had been leading them (and myself) to that conclusion, even though I knew deep down that the more layers of that artifice that built up, the further I got from the truly important things.

So when I first realized after meeting Eugeo that I didn't have to pretend to be anything, I was amazed—and wondered why.

Because unlike me, Eugeo had an artificial fluctlight? Because he didn't know Kirito the *SAO* hero? No, the greatest reason was that here in the Underworld, a place that was both real and false, Eugeo was blessed with far greater ability.

His natural talent for the sword was tremendous. Perception, decisiveness, reaction speed: I'd been fighting through plenty of VR worlds, but he was greater in all categories. If my fluctlight's battle processor was a current-model silicon CPU, then Eugeo's was a next-generation diamond CPU. I was still playing the role of instructor to him, but it was only because I had more experience and knowledge. If Eugeo kept improving at his current pace, it wouldn't be long before our positions were switched.

Like sand sucking up water, Eugeo had absorbed all the combat strategies I'd built up over the last few years, which I grandiosely called the Aincrad style. I couldn't help but feel a strangely deep joy and satisfaction in his progress. This swordplay had been the source of my personal pride, and yet nothing more than gaming techniques—and it felt like Eugeo learning and making them his own had turned that skill into something real for the first time.

If I could solve all the problems afflicting the Underworld and escape safely with Eugeo's fluctlight intact, I wanted to have him dive into *ALfheim Online* instead—I was certain that the lightcube was capable of interfacing with all Seed-based VR worlds equally—so that he could meet Asuna, Leafa, Klein, and all the others. *Here's my first pupil and best friend*, I'd say to them.

I couldn't wait for that moment to arrive. At that point, for the very first time, I'd finally be on the same level as the many people who supported and helped me…

"What are you grinning about?"

I blinked, startled out of my reverie by the sound of a voice to my right. I turned to see Alice, who was watching me with an unpleasant look. I quickly brought up a hand to rub at the corner of my mouth as I protested, "Er, I was just…thinking about some stuff ahead…"

"Based on the slack-jawed smile I was seeing, you're either a tremendous optimist or a tremendous idiot. At a time when our escape from this stone ledge is far from guaranteed."

The respite of our perch had not dulled her tongue. I wasn't familiar with the Alice from Rulid, who was the original basis for Alice the knight, but if her personality was like this after being restored, I could easily foresee a situation back in the real world, post-escape with Eugeo, where she'd clash with some of the more stubborn members of our group, like Sinon and Lisbeth.

On the other hand, there was still a veritable mountain of problems to solve before I even got close to that ultimate good ending. Our first order of business was to escape this terrace with its creepy minion statues, but not only was I still waiting for the spatial resources needed to generate more climbing hooks; my own mental and physical resources—such as my gurgling empty stomach—were also rapidly reaching their limit.

I nonchalantly rubbed my belly with a hand as I composed the most serious expression I could. "I think we'll be able to resume climbing when the moon is up. It's not too hard of a process as long as I can make those wedges. It doesn't seem like there are more minions up above…The biggest problem, as I see it, is that I'm so hungry, even the thought of climbing this sheer wall another few dozen mels is making me dizzy…"

"…It's that side of you that displays your lack of discipline. So you missed a meal or two. Are you really such a child that you cannot function at all without it?"

"Yeah, yeah, I'm just a kid, blah-blah-blah. I happen to be smack in the middle of my growth period. And unlike you fancy Integrity Knights, I actually lose life if I don't eat regularly."

"Just so you're aware, Integrity Knights feel hunger, and we lose life if we do not eat, too!" Alice snapped back.

At that moment, a cute, high-pitched squeak emitted from her midsection, and I couldn't stop myself from chuckling. Instantly, her face went red and her hand snapped over to the hilt of her sword.

I scrambled backward about fifty cens and stammered, "W-wait, I'm sorry, I'm sorry! You're right—you're just as alive as anyone else. Of course you get hungry, too."

I hunched myself smaller, and in the process noticed the sensation of something moving in my left pocket. When I touched it, I instantly recognized the texture and thanked my past preparation and stubborn greediness.

"Ooh! Manna from Heaven. Look what I've got here."

I pulled out two steamed buns. I'd stuck them in my pocket before we left Cardinal's library. Eugeo and I ate half of them earlier in the day, but I'd completely forgotten about the other two. They were a bit impacted by all the fierce combat earlier, but I wasn't going to complain.

"...Why did you have those in your pocket?" Alice asked, looking utterly annoyed by this sudden revelation.

"Tap your pocket, and you get two buns," I said cryptically, referencing a children's song that I was certain Alice wouldn't understand, then displayed the buns' window to ensure they had enough life to guarantee safety. They looked shabby now, but Cardinal had crafted them from some very high-value tomes in her library, and their durability rating was astonishingly high as a result.

Still, a cold, hard steamed bun wasn't going to be tasty the way it was. After a bit of thought, I spread my fingers and chanted, "System Call. Generate Thermal Element."

There wasn't enough magical power in the air for a full

climbing hook, but there was for one little bit of heat. A flickering bit of light appeared over my palm. I moved it closer to the buns in my other hand and said, "Bur..."

But before I could finish the word *burst*, the knight's hand shot over my mouth, as quick as lightning.

"—Mmph?!"

"Are you utterly stupid?! You'll be charred to a crisp!" she snapped, eyes full of fury and annoyance and disdain. She snatched the food from my hand. I moaned in disappointment, right as the tiny heat element evaporated.

The knight didn't even look at me as she zipped her hand and recited, in singsong fashion, "Generate Aerial Element...Thermal Element...Aqueous Element."

Between her thumb, index, and middle fingers appeared lights of orange, blue, and green. To my befuddlement, Alice then continued the command and manipulated the three elements in complex ways. First the wind element formed a spherical vortex, inside of which she floated the two buns. Next she added the heat and water elements, and when all three were mixed, she unleashed them.

With a little *fssh!* the wind barrier soon turned pure white. It looked quaint and peaceful, but I knew that inside, it was a swirl of heat and steam. In other words, she had constructed an impromptu steaming device.

Thirty seconds later, the trio of elements had concluded its duty, and it expanded until disappearing. The buns fell into Alice's outstretched hand, as puffed and round as if they were brand-new, and wafting steam.

"H-h-here, give it— Wha...Whaaaa—?!" I wailed as Alice made to devour both of the steamed buns before I could so much as reach out to them. She stopped just before they reached her mouth and said, in a tone that suggested dead seriousness, "I'm joking." Then she handed me one, which I took with great relief and blew on before taking a hefty bite.

I understood that everything in the Underworld was a kind of dream object taken from a vast collection of memories—but even still, the soft, steamed bun and juicy, succulent meat sent me into a brief state of nirvana. It took just three bites for the precious food to vanish into my stomach—or more accurately, return to the fluctlight memory field—leaving me with just a combination of satisfaction, disappointment, and one very hearty sigh.

It took Alice four bites to devour her bun, and she exhaled the same way I did. I was struck that the Integrity Knight, practically an avatar of pure battle, could have such a girlish side.

"Ah, I see," I remarked. "You can steam a bun without even any tools. I guess it makes sense that you'd be Selka's sister, after how good she was at cooki—"

Midsentence, a hand shot out and grabbed my collar. This time, it was not annoyance or disgust that marked Alice's features. Those blue eyes were furious as exploding sparks, her cheeks were pale, and her lips were trembling. She practically hoisted me up with nothing but her right hand and rasped, "What…did you just say?"

Only then, at that belated moment, did I finally recognize my terrible slip of the tongue.

The golden-haired Integrity Knight staring a hole in me from less than a foot away was none other than Alice Zuberg, Eugeo's childhood friend and sister to the apprentice nun Selka—but she herself had no memory of this. Eight years ago she was taken to Centoria and subjected to the Synthesis Ritual that made her into an Integrity Knight by taking away her most precious memory and installing a Piety Module that blocked the rest.

As far as she knew now, Alice was a knight summoned from Heaven to uphold the peace and order of the realm and fight against invasions from the darkness. According to what had been implanted in her mind, the Axiom Church and its ruler, Administrator, were all-powerful and trustworthy. She would never believe the truth: that Administrator was finding promising people around the world and transforming them into her pawns to uphold her own power and greed.

In fact, it was because we could sense that talk alone would not convince Alice that Eugeo and I planned to use Cardinal's special daggers to temporarily paralyze her. We certainly didn't plan on the current situation, but my objective remained the same: avoid fighting Alice, regroup with Eugeo, and create an opportunity for him to use his dagger on her.

Sensing that I could have destroyed that plan with one ill-timed slip, my mind raced for a solution. The expression on her face made it clear that I couldn't wriggle out of this by claiming I had misspoken.

It seemed there were only two options. I could either fight Alice here, knock her out without killing her, and carry her up to the ninetieth floor—or I could suck it up and tell her everything.

My choice would depend on what I believed about her. If I believed her skill with the sword was below mine, I should choose battle. If I believed she could be reasoned with, I should choose dialogue.

A few seconds of deliberation later, I made my choice. With the full might of Alice's flaming blue eyes upon me, I said, "You have a sister. I'll explain...I don't know if you'll believe it, but I will tell you everything I believe to be the truth."

However this statement struck her, Alice mulled it over for several seconds and then released me. I dropped flat on my butt onto the stone, where the knight looked down on me from her kneeling position. Even hearing me out in this situation seemed like it was outside the bounds of an Integrity Knight's activities. She was locked in a battle between her logical duty to vanquish me with her blade and the desire to know what was unknown.

Eventually, desire won out. She slowly lowered herself to a proper sitting position and hissed, "Speak. But be warned...if I sense that your words are meant to mislead me, I will not hesitate to cut you in two."

I sucked in a long breath and held it. "That's fine...if your decision to attack me comes from your own true heart. And the reason I say that is because inside of you is an order that was implanted in you by someone else, an order you're not aware of."

"…Are you speaking of the Integrity Knight's duty?"

"That's right," I said. Alice's eyes narrowed with hostility. But I could detect an emotional hesitation lurking behind them. That would be Alice's true feelings. I hoped that my words would break through to that part of her.

"Integrity Knights are summoned from the celestial realm by Administrator, the pontifex of the Axiom Church, in order to maintain order and justice…or so you understand. But only the people here within Central Cathedral actually think that. The thousands and thousands of people living across the realm don't see it that way."

"What…nonsense are you talking about…?"

"Go down there to the city and ask anyone in Centoria what the prize is for the winner of the annual Four-Empire Unification Tournament. They'll tell you that the winner receives the honor of being made an Integrity Knight."

"Made into…an Integrity Knight…? That's nonsense. That can't be right. I've interacted with many of the knights, and not a single one has ever said they were a human being before that."

"It's just the opposite. Not a single one of you started as anything other than human," I said, back straight, staring her right in the eyes. I was desperately trying to break through to that human part of her, deep inside. "Alice, you don't know who gave birth to you in the 'celestial realm,' or where you were raised. I'd bet your oldest active memory is Administrator telling you that you are a holy knight summoned from Heaven."

"…"

I was correct, judging by her reaction. She leaned back just a little and bit her lip. "I…was told…that when an Integrity Knight is summoned to earth, Stacia removes her memories of Heaven… and that when the evil ones of the Dark Territory are vanquished, and I have completed my duty as a knight, I will be returned to the holy place…and remember my parents and siblings again… according to…the pontifex…"

Her normally crisp voice faltered and trailed away. Suddenly I knew. Somewhere deep in Alice's heart, in a place she wasn't aware of, she was desperate for her family memories. That must have been why she had reacted so powerfully to the mention of Selka's name.

Choosing my words carefully, I explained, "Only a part of what Administrator told you is true. Yes, your memories were kept from you. But it wasn't because of Stacia; it was the pontifex herself who did it. And it's not your heavenly memories that are hidden but your human memories, of being born and raised here. It's the same for all the other Integrity Knights, too, like Eldrie. He's the son of a noble house in the Norlangarth Empire. He won the tournament this year and earned the honor of being made into a knight."

"No…that's a lie! My apprentice, Knight Thirty-One, could not be a descendent of the decadent nobles…"

"Listen to me: When we defeated Eldrie in combat, it wasn't because we killed him. Did you see any major wounds on him? My partner remembered his real name, Eldrie Woolsburg, and that stimulated his memories of his mother. He wanted to remember her, but he couldn't. That was because Administrator took that memory out of his soul and keeps it at the very top of the cathedral."

"…His memory…of his mother…?" she murmured, lips trembling. Her eyes were wandering on empty air. "Eldrie's…noble… human…mother…?"

"And that doesn't just go for him. I'd bet at least half the knights are champions of the swordfighting tournament, and the majority of those would be noble children who were raised with the best possible education with the blade. The noble houses receive considerable wealth and status from turning their children over to the Axiom Church. That system has been in place for over a century now."

"...I can't believe it...I just cannot accept the story you are telling me," the Integrity Knight said, shaking her head like a stubborn child at the notion that the Axiom Church and its knights weren't utterly divine. "Not all the upper nobles in the four empires are like this, but many lead slothful and decadent lives. It is why we Integrity Knights are necessary to protect the human lands. And now you claim...that Eldrie and others in the knighthood...are actually from those degenerate noble houses...? It is not possible. I cannot believe it."

"The reason those noble families are decadent is because the Axiom Church gave them too much prestige and power. But because of that privilege, their children grow up with excellent instruction in swordplay and sacred arts. In rural villages, children are given their callings at age ten and barely ever have time to practice fighting with swords, by comparison. And only the most gifted of those noble children can appear in the Four-Empire Unification Tournament, and the single champion of that event is invited to Central Cathedral. Have you ever met one of those champions within the cathedral?" I asked.

Alice looked away, uncertain, and shook her head. "No...but there are many monks, nuns, and their apprentices living on the lower floors...so perhaps those champions are down among them, enriching their lives through study..."

I nearly spoke up on the spot to deny that but thought better of it. Eugeo and I had come straight up the stairs to the fiftieth floor after we'd retrieved our swords from the cathedral's third floor—with only the distraction of the child knights Fizel and Linel around the twentieth floor—and we hadn't encountered any of the holy workers. But I could still speculate about their source.

My suspicion was that the majority of the monks and nuns undertaking the basic duties of the Axiom Church weren't hired from the outside but were born and raised within the Church, just like Fizel and Linel. Administrator probably viewed them like practical-use production models she could replicate.

Alice wouldn't know about that dark side of the organization, I figured. I didn't need to bring up the idea and tax her mind more than necessary.

"No, you've met champions of the tournament. You're just not aware of it. All the Integrity Knights' memories are being manipulated and adjusted by Administrator on a constant basis, not just during the ritual."

"Nonsense!" she shouted, raising her head. "That is impossible! The holy pontifex would never toy with our memories the way you describe…"

"She is!" I shouted back. "You're not just missing your memories of the tournament champions…You also don't remember the criminals you've brought back to the tower!"

"C-criminals…?" she said, faltering. I stared right into her face, which was pale even in the moonlight.

"That's right. Yesterday morning, you brought my partner and me here on your dragon from Swordcraft Academy. You remember that, don't you?"

"…I would not forget it. You were the first ones I have ever been ordered to escort to prison."

"Yet, Deusolbert Synthesis Seven didn't remember you. When eight years ago…"

I paused, then steeled myself to say the name.

"…he was the one who took young Alice from Rulid Village in the far north, himself."

She went whiter than the marble wall. Her bloodless lips quivered, and she croaked, "Rulid…That's my true hometown…? And Deusolbert escorted me from there as a criminal…? In other words, I once violated a taboo…? Is that what you are saying?"

I waited for her to finish each and every question. "That's right. Remember how I said half the Integrity Knights were tournament champions? The other half are people who were brought to the cathedral as criminals. They had the force of will to violate the Taboo Index, and that gives them exceptional power as knights. It's two birds with one stone for Administrator: She turns a potential threat to the Church's rule into a powerful personal agent. Now…let's talk about you."

This was it. The moment Alice would either accept my argument or deny it.

I fixed her with as firm a stare as I could possibly muster. She sat flat on the stone ledge, her shoulders hunched and forlorn, eyelids heavy, as though waiting for some final judgment.

"Your real name is Alice Zuberg. You were born and raised in Rulid, a small village at the foot of the End Mountains far to the north. You're the same age as Eugeo, my partner, which would make you nineteen this year. You were brought here eight years ago, meaning you were eleven when the incident happened. You and Eugeo went spelunking in the cave through the End Mountains…and at the other end of the cave, you just barely crossed the boundary between the human realm and the Dark Territory. So the taboo you broke was 'infiltrating the Dark Territory.' You didn't steal anything or hurt anyone…In fact, you were trying to save the dying dark knight…"

Now it was my turn to clam up. Did I really hear that many details about Alice's story from Eugeo…?

Surely I did. I awoke in the Underworld two years ago—I couldn't possibly know what happened six years before that. But for some reason, there was an image in my brain of a knight in black falling from the sky in a shower of blood and Alice rushing toward him, as vivid and specific as if I'd seen it myself. I even heard the scraping sound of her hand brushing the black soil of the Dark Territory.

Somehow, the imagery of Eugeo's story must have gotten mixed up with my memories from reality, I told myself. I looked up and saw that Alice was so shaken by all this that she wasn't bothered by the way I trailed off. Her cheeks were sallow, twitching.

"Alice Zuberg," she whispered. "That's…my…name? Rulid… End Mountains…I can't remember any of it…"

"Don't force yourself to remember, or you'll end up like Eldrie," I warned, cutting her off. If Alice's Piety Module turned unstable and stopped working like his, there might be trouble—especially if the other knights sensed it happening and came to get her. But Alice merely looked at me with slightly more control than a moment before.

"Why would you say that now?" she demanded, her voice trembling. "I…I want to know everything. I don't believe what you've said yet…but I will make my decision on that once I've heard the whole story."

"All right. But to be honest, I don't know that much about your past. Your dad is the elder of Rulid, Gasfut Zuberg. I don't know your mother's name, unfortunately, but like I said earlier, you have a little sister named Selka, who is probably still a sister-in-training at the church in Rulid. When I stayed there two years ago, I talked with her a lot. She was a good kid, and she cared about her sister; she'd been worried about you ever since you were taken away. When you lived in Rulid, you were also an apprentice and were considered to have a genius talent for sacred arts. She was trying her hardest to inherit that position and take over for you in your absence."

That was all I knew. Alice said nothing for a while. Her earlier unrest was gone now, and that porcelain-white face was utterly still. She seemed to be trying to dredge up anything she could remember about those proper names, but it wasn't producing any results.

It didn't work, I realized. I'd been hoping that even without that missing memory fragment, if I calmly gave her bits of relevant information, she'd eventually recall some of those memories. Evidently, Administrator's memory block was stronger than I realized.

The only one who could restore Alice was Cardinal, who had admin privileges. And that would still require the missing memory fragment that Administrator was keeping locked up.

Just then, Alice's mouth opened.

"Selka."

She did it again.

"Selka..."

Her darkened eyes pointed to the stars overhead.

"...I can't remember. No face, no voice. But...it's not the first time I've said that name. My mouth...my throat...my heart remembers."

"...Alice," I said, but she didn't seem to even be aware I was there anymore.

"I called it all the time," she whispered. "Every day, every night...Selka...Selka...Sel..."

Clear drops clung to her long lashes, sparkling with the light of the stars before they fell. I felt like I was seeing something unbelievable. The tears kept coming and coming, dripping with tiny patters onto the marble between us.

"It's true...I have a family...a father and mother...and a sister I share blood with...somewhere out there under these stars...," she choked, until her voice turned to sobs.

Before I knew what I was doing, I had reached out to her, but she batted me away with the back of her hand.

"Don't look at me!" she sobbed, smacking me in the chest with her right hand while she rubbed at her eyes with the left. The tears never stopped, however, and eventually she buried her face in her knees, shoulders shaking.

"Nng...hnk...aaah..."

As the Integrity Knight continued to quietly sob, I came to the realization that liquid was pooling in my eyes as well.

I'll do it. I'll stop this Administrator and take Alice back home, I swore, my mission renewed, as I understood what was making me emotional, too.

Even if the plan went successfully, it wouldn't be this sobbing Integrity Knight whom I reunited with Selka in Rulid. Alice would recover her lost memories, remember how she grew up with Eugeo and Selka, and probably forget about her years of service as a knight.

That would essentially be the destruction of Alice the Integrity Knight.

She'd be returning to the way she ought to be, I reminded myself. But I couldn't help but feel pity for the weeping knight curled up in a miserable ball.

For all the years she had spent at Central Cathedral, Alice Synthesis Thirty had been pained by the deep, subconscious desire for the company of the family she could never see again. I couldn't help but sympathize.

Eventually, much later, her racking sobs subsided in volume, to be replaced by silent weeping. My own tears had already dried a few minutes before that, so I decided to focus on what should happen next.

If there was an ideal outcome out of anything I could reasonably envision, it would be as follows: Once the moon rose, we'd resume climbing and reenter the tower at the ninety-fifth floor. Somehow, I would avoid resuming battle with Alice there and meet up with Eugeo again. Whether or not we used Cardinal's special dagger in his possession would depend on the circumstances.

After that, the biggest obstacle remaining would be to defeat Bercouli Synthesis One or persuade him not to fight us. It would be great if Eugeo had already beaten him, but I couldn't count on that. Then we'd reach the top floor of the cathedral, where our ultimate foe, Administrator, slept.

We'd have to neutralize the pontifex before she awoke, find Alice's memory fragment, wherever it was hidden in the chamber, then use it to restore her memories and personality.

Lastly, I'd use the system console to make contact with the Rath staff, preserve the state of the Underworld, and get them to prevent the imminent stress test—a massive invasion from the Dark Territory...

Each one of these missions was astonishingly difficult; all of them together was hard to fathom. I had to assume that each individual goal had a probability of 50 percent, if not 30 or lower.

But I wasn't allowed to stop in my tracks now. The two years I'd spent in the Underworld—in fact, the very long time ever since I'd first been locked in that game of death—had all been leading up to this encounter with a new kind of humanity so I could save them.

As Akihiko Kayaba had stared at the collapsing Aincrad against the red of the sunset, he'd claimed he wanted to create a truly alternate world. I wasn't carrying on his mission, not in the least, but I had to admit that a true alternate world was exactly what I was seeing here.

Kayaba's digital copy left The Seed with me, and it ultimately brought about an infinite array of VR worlds across the Internet. And whether by fate or by coincidence, the lightcube format that stored the souls of the Underworldians was compatible with The Seed Nexus. If there was some greater meaning to the *SAO* Incident beyond whatever Kayaba hoped to achieve, I got the feeling I would find it here in the Underworld.

I couldn't turn back now. Two long years after I woke up in the forest south of Rulid, I was finally bearing down on the last floor of Central Cathedral, the goal of my long journey. But if there was any tiny but unavoidable problem along the way, it was that out of those many laudable goals, there was just one I wasn't entirely certain I wanted to achieve…

"…A while ago, you mentioned something," Alice said abruptly, looking down with her arms wrapped around her knees.

I abandoned the tangle of thoughts I was trying to unravel and looked over at her.

A few moments later, she continued, voice slightly nasal from being blocked up. "After the wall broke, and we fell through it… you said you planned this rebellion in order to correct the pontifex's mistake and protect the human world."

"Yeah…that's right," I said, noticing the blond hair that fell down Alice's back.

After several seconds of silence, she continued, "I do not believe…everything you've said yet. But…with the minions of the lands of darkness on the outside of the tower…I must admit that your claim that the Integrity Knights are just regular human beings with their memories manipulated seems to be true. In other words…I cannot deny that our master has been deeply deceiving us in order to make us her faithful servants…"

I held my breath. By removing their memories and inserting the Piety Module into the fluctlight of the Integrity Knights, Administrator forced them to be absolutely loyal warriors. No matter what Eugeo and I said to any of the knights we'd met thus far, none had expressed a single word of doubt toward the Church. In that sense, it should've been stunning to me that Alice said what she did. Perhaps she had something in her that the other artificial fluctlights did not.

She didn't undo the grip around her upright knees as she whispered, "But on the other hand, our primary duty as commanded by the pontifex is to protect against an invasion from the Dark Territory. Even now, more than a dozen of my fellow knights are riding their dragons, fighting over the End Mountains. If she hadn't created the Integrity Knights, the dark forces would have invaded our lands long ago."

"Ah, well…"

…*That's because this isn't the way the world is supposed to work.*

Those growth resources—i.e., experience points—the Integrity Knights were monopolizing were supposed to be distributed throughout the populace. The people of the realm should have taken up swords and fought against invading goblins, the same way Eugeo and I did in the northern cave, to get stronger. Administrator had taken that possibility away from them.

Alice wouldn't understand that on the spot, though. Instead, I had to hold back my rebuttal as she continued, quiet but firm, "You claim that my birth home, the place where my parents and sister must still live, is at the foot of the mountains to the far north. In other words, if an invasion begins, they would be the first to fall victim. Even if you defeat all the Integrity Knights and turn your blades on the pontifex herself, who will protect all the distant rural villages like Rulid? You don't expect to vanquish the entire forces of darkness just with the two of you, I hope."

The tears in her eyes weren't totally dry yet, but there was a newfound willpower in her voice. Still, I couldn't give her an answer right away. Compared to Alice's open determination to save the people of the world, I still had secrets to hide.

I had to fight the sudden urge to truly spill it all and explain that this entire world was a creation. Instead I said, "Then let me ask you this…If you fight with the full might of the Integrity Knights, do you believe that you can absolutely, without fail, fight off an all-out invasion from the Dark Territory?"

"…"

Now it was Alice's turn to be at a loss for words. I looked back to the stars and traveled the memories I'd built over the last two years.

"I told you about how my partner and I battled a band of goblins from the Dark Territory. Even those goblins, the lowest members of the forces of darkness, were frightfully skilled and powerful with their weapons. The Dark Territory is full of them, and those dragon-riding black knights, and dark sorcerers controlling their own minions, right? If they all attack at once, then even with all the Integrity Knights together, plus Administrator, you're not going to be able to hold back the tide."

The vast majority of this information was just repeating what Cardinal had told me, but Alice seemed to accept it as fact in stride; she didn't bite back the way she often did. After a few moments of reflection, she murmured, "It's true that Uncle…er, Commander Bercouli seems to have his own doubts. The Dark Territory already has tens of thousands of elite forces, and if they breach the eastern gate all at once, even the knights may not be able to keep up…But on the other hand, there is essentially no other worthwhile power in the human realm aside from ours. You mentioned that the children of elite noble houses receive special training in the sword and sacred arts—but their skill is aesthetic in nature and not suited to true battle. We will simply have to work together, with the few dragons we have, and trust in the blessings of the three goddesses. You understand the situation, don't you?"

"You're correct…There's nothing here to counteract the armies of darkness aside from the Integrity Knights," I said, gazing straight ahead. "But that's a situation that Administrator created by design. Your pontifex was afraid of any kind of power that threatened her absolute rule over the Human Empire. That's why she gathered tournament champions and rebels against the Taboo Index, removed their memories, and rebuilt them into faithful knights. Or to put it another way, Administrator does not have an ounce of trust in the people of this world."

"…!"

Alice sucked in a sharp breath. Once again, she didn't have an instant rebuttal. Praying that I'd struck a nerve deep in her soul, I continued, "If she trusted the people who live here, she would form well-equipped militias and allow them to train, and perhaps there would be a battle force capable of countering the Dark Territory's now. But she didn't do that. She allowed the higher nobles—the people who should be first to fight if a war erupts—to be slothful and decadent. Now their souls are corrupted…just like the two Eugeo and I attacked at the academy."

Raios Antinous and Humbert Zizek's attempted rape of Tiese and Ronie was just two days ago. If the stress test arrived and the Dark Territory invaded the human realm, scenes like that would occur everywhere, in horrifying numbers.

"But it's not too late to do anything about it yet. I don't know how much time we have until the Dark Territory invades, whether it's one year or two…but if we can arrange a large human army by then, perhaps…"

"We can do no such thing!" Alice cried. "You just said it yourself. The nobles are all craven and corrupt! If a war begins and the four imperial houses and nobles are called upon to take their swords and fight, they will oblige only in name and ensure that their lives and fortunes are kept intact!"

"You're right that most of the higher nobles have no real intention of fighting. But some do have their pride, and among the lower nobles and common people, there are those with the will to protect their families and towns…and this world as a whole. If the wealth of weapons stored in this tower is distributed to them and you folks teach them your true swordfighting and sacred arts, it's not unthinkable that we could have a proper army built up within a year."

"The common…people…?" she repeated.

"That's right," I said. "Even if we just take volunteers rather than conscripting an army, we should be able to build quite a crowd. There are already guard garrisons in the towns and villages all over. The problem is…at this point, such a strategy is impossible to employ."

"Because…the pontifex…would never allow it…"

"Right. We couldn't even persuade her based on its wisdom. An army that can't be forced into absolute servitude is just as terrifying to Administrator as the forces of darkness are. That leaves just one conclusion: We must break Administrator's absolute rule, effectively use what time we have left, and build a defensive force for the upcoming invasion," I declared, but I couldn't help but feel irony in that statement.

Rath, the company behind the Underworld, had a close connection to Seijirou Kikuoka, an officer with the nation's Self-Defense Force. That meant this entire operation had to have deep ties to national security in the real world. Perhaps they even meant to utilize artificial fluctlights like Eugeo and Alice to control their weapons of war.

I couldn't possibly condone such a thing, and yet I was arguing that tens of thousands of civilians should be turned into soldiers for a massive war.

Alice had no idea of this inner dilemma; she was silent for her own reasons. No doubt she was balancing a scale with her soul-etched loyalty to the Axiom Church on one side, and on the other, the words of the intruder she'd escorted here by her own hand. Her expression was controlled, but I knew I couldn't fathom the true depth of her anguish and indecision.

Eventually, I heard a brief phrase on the night breeze.

"…see her?"

"What…?"

"If I help you…and we regain my hidden memories, will I be able to see Selka…my sister again?"

I had to clench my jaw. She could do it. Of course she could see her. But…

I wasn't sure whether I should relate my earlier prediction, but the last thing I wanted to do just then was mince words. I steeled myself and said, "Yes…you will. If you use your dragon, it will only take a day or two. But there's something you need to hear first…"

I stared right into Alice's eyes, about four feet to my right, and continued, "It's not exactly you who will be reuniting with Selka. The moment you get your memory back, you'll return to being Alice Zuberg from before the Synthesis Ritual, and Alice Synthesis Thirty will cease to be. You'll lose your memories of being an Integrity Knight and return this body to its rightful persona. It's cruel to say, but…the you right now is a false Alice created by Administrator."

Her shoulders trembled at various points as I spoke. But there were no more sobs. Seconds later, she spoke in a voice with all emotion restrained.

"Once you told me…that the Integrity Knights were a creation of the pontifex…I had a feeling this might be the case. That I stole this body from a girl named Alice Zuberg…and have monopolized it for six long years."

I had no idea what to say to this. No doubt she had a storm of feelings, but Alice only gave me a brave smile. "I must return what I have stolen. That would be the wish of Selka…her parents… your friend…and you, I suspect."

"…Alice…"

"But…I have just one request."

"Which is…?"

"Before you return this body to the persona of the original Alice…will you take me to Rulid? And then, in secret…I wish to see Selka, my sister…and my family. If you can do that for me, I will be happy."

She ended there and slowly turned her head to look at me. In that very instant, the moon cast a ray of light between the clouds to the east. With her entire outline framed in golden beams, Alice's red and swollen eyes softened, and she smiled just a bit. I couldn't take it and had to look up at the moon.

We'd get Alice's memory back. That was the only thing that Eugeo truly wanted—and therefore, what I wanted as well.

But it would also be a death sentence for the Integrity Knight—no, the young woman—clenching her knees next to me. An unavoidable sacrifice, and an inescapable set of priorities. I couldn't do anything about it.

"Yes…I promise. I swear to you," I said, eyes to the sky. "I'll take you to Rulid before we return the memories."

"…You'd better," she warned. I looked at her and nodded. She returned the gesture, took a deep breath, and put on a brave face. "All right, then. In order to protect the realm…and all the people within it, I, Alice Synthesis Thirty, hereby abandon my title and rank of Integrity Kni— *Aah!!*"

Her proclamation quickly turned to a shriek. Her golden armor rattled as she bolted backward and covered her right eye. Devastating pain twisted her beautiful features.

I was momentarily stunned into rising off my seat, until I recalled an incident from a few days prior.

Eugeo had cut off the arm of Humbert Zizek to save Ronie and Tiese, and by the time I'd reached him, his right eye had blown clear out of its socket, and tears of vivid blood were spurting down his cheek.

In the school's detention cell that night, Eugeo had described what he'd felt. The moment he tried to attack Humbert, his arm went cold and dead as if it didn't belong to him, and his right eye burned with agony. Floating in front of him were bright-red, unfamiliar sacred letters…

Alice had to have been experiencing the same phenomenon. It was some kind of mental block, I suspected, triggered whenever the individual tried to fight against the orders carved into her soul.

"Don't think about anything! Shut off your mind!" I shouted as I approached, holding down her left shoulder. With my other hand, I grabbed her wrist and forced it away from her right eye.

"…?!"

Alice's sapphire-blue eye was no longer the same—instead, there was a blinking red tint to it. I gasped and leaned in to get a better look.

Along the edge of Alice's circular blue iris, there was a series of fine, radiating red lines that rotated slowly. They weren't of equal width, and their arrangement looked random. It was almost like…a bar code.

Ever since Eugeo had described what had happened to him, I'd assumed it was Administrator who'd installed this mental block on the Underworldians. But I couldn't ever recall seeing anything resembling a bar code during my two years there.

*So this…*isn't *Administrator's doing…? But then, who…?*

I gasped.

The circular bar code stopped rotating, and a strange string of symbols passed over Alice's contracted pupils. The bright-red series of letters looked like TЯƎ⅃A MƎTƧYƧ.

For a moment, I was unsure how to read them—until I realized they were mirrored. Alice's retina was on the other side of the letters, so their direction was reversed from her point of view. The letters spelled out SYSTEM ALERT.

It was a phrase I was long familiar with from using PCs, typically accompanied by an unpleasant dinging sound. That phrase should have no meaning to Alice and the Underworldians, though. In their lives, all Japanese words were considered the "common language," while English was known as the "sacred tongue." Hardly any of the citizens actually understood the definition of the words; they considered them unnecessary.

When learning sacred arts, the initial System Call and its subsequent English commands were essentially treated like sounds, and their meanings were ignored. When I taught Eugeo the various sword skills that I identified as special techniques of the Aincrad style, he always marveled that I understood things about the sacred tongue.

So this SYSTEM ALERT warning was meaningless to the Underworldians. That meant the mental block installed in Alice and Eugeo wasn't from Administrator but from people in the real world—members of Rath's staff...

Alice let out a high-pitched scream right in my face, cutting off my thoughts. "My...my eye, it's burning...! And I...I see some kind...of writing!"

"Don't think! Empty your mind!!" I shouted, placing my hands on either side of her dainty face. "What's happening to you now is a kind of mental barrier that happens to those who try to defy the Church. It's causing that pain in your eye in an attempt to enforce your unconditional obedience...If you keep thinking about that, your eye's going to burst!"

Unfortunately, given the circumstances, the more I warned her, the more it could backfire. No human being was so in control of their mind that they could stop thinking about something on command.

Alice squeezed her eyelids shut. But that wasn't going to remove the red letters superimposed over her eye. Her hands floated out into the air and clutched at me when they brushed my shoulder. With each little shriek of pain, more and more force was pressed through her fingers, making my bones and muscles creak. But I knew that my suffering was nothing compared to hers.

I applied pressure to her face with my palms, hoping that it might at least calm her thoughts a bit. In the background, I desperately considered the turn of events.

Several of the Integrity Knights, including Alice, had already broken a taboo before. I knew that because it was how they'd been brought before the Axiom Church and given the Synthesis Ritual.

But in Alice's case, there had been no splitting pain in her right eye when she committed the crime of trespassing into the Dark Territory eight years ago—at least, nothing compared to Eugeo's. According to him, Alice crossed the boundary line without even realizing it. In other words, at the moment of the violation, her mind had no conscious understanding or intent to break that taboo.

Most likely, the mental barrier she was suffering was a reaction to intentionally trying to break a taboo. The instant she got the idea, the pain in her eye started, followed by the SYSTEM ALERT warning, to instill fear of the taboo. As obedient as the Underworldians already were by nature, this magic-seeming mental block had to be sufficient to keep them almost perfectly subservient.

However, if the mental barrier was the work of Rath's employees, that created one very significant paradox. The purpose of the Underworld test was, I suspected, to create artificial fluctlights that could break rules—or more accurately, that could judge a constructed morality system for themselves. If you had an Underworldian close to a breakthrough, what would be the point of a crude, violent mental block that forces them backward?

Wouldn't that mean whoever constructed this alert system was intentionally delaying the success of the experiment? Who would such a person be, and what was the point?

I briefly considered the replicated persona of Heathcliff, Akihiko Kayaba, but cast that aside. He wished for the creation of a true alternate world, so he wouldn't interfere with the evolution of the artificial fluctlights. And this sort of forceful handiwork wasn't his style. Perhaps it was some kind of group or individual hostile to Rath, performing sabotage.

If Seijirou Kikuoka was running Rath as an SDF officer, I could imagine any number of hostile forces. There could be some other internal group opposed to Kikuoka's project, a major military company trying to maintain a stranglehold on the defense industry, perhaps even some foreign weapons manufacturer or intelligence agency.

But if such powerful forces were involved in sabotaging Rath, would they really go to these subtle and particular lengths? If they had enough power to install a sabotage routine in the artificial fluctlights, surely it would be easier just to destroy the lightcube cluster itself and be done with it?

In other words, the intention of this mystery saboteur was merely to delay the project, not shut it down entirely. Were they waiting for something to happen? Some massive counterproject that required plenty of time to prepare? Perhaps…

The theft of the complete experiment results, including the lightcube cluster. A chill ran through my hands as they held Alice, who suddenly wailed, "How cruel…"

I came back to my senses and glanced at her. Those graceful eyebrows were twisted in pain, little droplets sat at the corners of her eyes, and she'd bitten her lip so hard, it was bleeding.

That lip trembled, the skin pale, as she continued, "How cruel…to have…not just my memories…but even my mind manipulated…by someone else…" Her hands on my shoulders trembled, out of either sadness or anger. "Was it…the pontifex… who burned this red sacred script…into my eyes…?"

"No…I don't think it was," I admitted on the spot. "It's one of the powers who created this world and observes it from the outside… One of the gods that don't appear in your creation story."

"…Gods." Clear drops fell from her eyes without a sound. "We knights engage in endless battle to protect the world the gods created…and yet, they do not have faith in us? They take my memories of family away, then place this terrible hex on me…to force my servitude…"

Alice lived her life as a holy knight—I couldn't imagine how much shock, disbelief, and despair she must have been feeling.

As I watched, my breath caught in my lungs as Alice's eyes bolted open.

The letters running across her right iris were still a brilliant red. But she stared right through the message into the sky—at the pale moon floating between the heavy clouds.

"I am not a puppet!" she announced, her voice clear and strong, if ragged around the edges. "Perhaps I was constructed. But I still have a will! I wish to protect this world...and the people in it! I wish to protect my parents! My sister! That is my primary duty!!"

With a high-pitched metallic whine, the letters on her eye glowed brighter. The rotating bar code around the edge of her iris sped up.

"Alice!" I cried, sensing what was about to happen.

Without looking back at me, she whispered, "Kirito...hold me down firmly."

"...Right."

There was nothing else I could do. I let go of Alice's face and moved my grip to her armored shoulders. Through the golden plate, I squeezed her tight as she trembled.

She gestured up to the sky, long golden hair waving, and sucked in a deep breath.

"Administrator...and you unnamed gods! For the sake of my mission...I swear to oppose you!!"

Her declaration of independence rang out, crisp and clear.

Barely a moment after the words left her mouth, the red glow in Alice's right eye surged into a burst of flame.

A spray of hot blood moistened my cheek.

2

Eugeo.
Eugeo…
What's wrong?
Did you have a bad dream…?

With a soft thrum, orange light filled the lamp.

Out in the hallway, Eugeo buried the bottom half of his face into the pillow in his arms and, without emerging from the darkness, peered through the slightly ajar door into the room.

It wasn't very big and featured two simple wooden beds. The one on the right was empty, its freshly washed blanket crisply folded. The bed on the left held a thin figure sitting upright, watching Eugeo. The face was hidden due to the light of the lamp in the figure's hand. The shining white pajama top was slightly open at the chest, revealing even whiter skin. The long hair that hung down to the bed looked as soft as silk.

Beyond the glow of the lamp, the only thing visible were her full lips, curled into a gentle smile.

It must be cold over there. Come here, Eugeo.

*   *   *

Underneath the covers, the bed was full of rich, warm, inviting darkness, which only served to remind him of the chilly breeze in the hallway. Just then, he was through the door, tottering toward the bed on uncertain legs.

For some reason, the closer he got, the weaker the lamplight became, and the darker the face of the woman on the bed. But Eugeo kept moving onward, driven by the desire to nestle into the pleasant darkness. His steps got shorter and shorter, and his viewpoint fell lower and lower, but he didn't find this strange.

When he reached the bed at last, it was terribly tall. He threw down his pillow and used it as a stepping stool to clamber up the side of the bed. Then a soft layer of cloth covered his head, plunging his vision into blackness. He crawled farther, farther into the dark, urged by a kind of primal longing.

His outstretched fingers brushed warm, soft skin. Eugeo clung to it, buried his face in it. The smooth skin wriggled and folded to welcome him in. Clinging to it brought him a numbing satisfaction, and twice as much longing. Smooth arms circled his back and brushed the top of his head.

"Mother…? Is that you, Mother?" he asked, his voice tiny.

The answer was immediate.

That's right…I'm your mother, Eugeo.

"Mother…my mother…," he mumbled, sinking deeper and deeper into the warm, clammy darkness. As his mind went dull and numb, one little piece of it raised a concern, as dull as an air bubble rising from a muddy swamp.

Was his Mother always so thin…and soft? She worked the barley fields every day—why were her hands so perfectly pristine? And…what had happened to his father, who should have been sleeping in the bed on the right? Where were all his brothers, who always got in the way when he sought comfort from this woman…?

＊　　＊　　＊

"Are you…really my mother?"

That's right, Eugeo. I'm your mother, and your mother alone.

"But…where's Father? Where did my brothers go?"

Ha-ha-ha.
Oh, you silly boy.
Remember?
You killed them all.

Suddenly, his fingers slid.
He held up his hands and spread them apart.
Even in the darkness, he could clearly see the bright-red color of blood dripping from his fingers.

"…Aaaaaahh!!" Eugeo screamed and bolted upright. He frantically rubbed his clammy hands against his shirt. After several shouts and much hasty friction, he finally realized that it was not blood smeared on his palms but sweat. He was lying on the ground in the fetal position.

It was just a dream. And yet, the wild beating of his heart and the sour sweat exuding from his skin showed no signs of calming. The remnants of a horrifying nightmare stayed stuck to his back, chilling and unpleasant.

I've hardly even thought of Mom and Dad since I left home, he realized, then clenched his eyes shut and panted. Back in Rulid, his mother was so busy with fieldwork, taking care of the sheep, and doing all the housework that she hardly ever had time to dote on Eugeo like that. At the time of his oldest memories, he was already sleeping in his own bed, and he'd never had a problem with it.

So why would I have a dream like that now…?
He shook his head, trying to dispel the vision. A person's

dreams were decided by the whims of Lunaria, the moon goddess. There was no meaning to that nightmare, surely.

Once his breathing was steady again, his mind turned to the question of where he was. Without uncurling his body, he lifted his eyelids.

The first thing he saw was a dark-red, stunningly deep carpet, woven with an intricate design. He couldn't begin to guess what the textile merchants in District Five of North Centoria would charge for such an item. He gradually raised his head, but there was no end to the carpet. Only when his head was fully level did he finally see a wall in the distance.

The "wall" wasn't wood paneled or made of stone blocks. It was an arrangement of golden pillars made to look like gigantic swords, connected by massive sheets of glass. That made it less of a wall than a very long, continuous window. In any case, he doubted that even the emperors' palaces made such decadent use of valuable glass.

Beyond the glass wall was a carpet of clouds glowing blue in the moonlight. So this chamber was located above the cloud layer. Hanging in the night sky above was a full white moon. A stunning canopy of stars sparkled around it. The rays of light coming down from the display above were so strong that Eugeo was late to realize it was still the middle of the night. Based on the position of the moon, it was probably just after midnight. So while he slept, the date changed, making it the twenty-fifth day of the fifth month now.

He looked straight up. Far above, the ceiling formed a perfect circle, with no sign of any staircase up to the next floor. Did that make this the very top floor of Central Cathedral?

There was a vivid painting on the vast ceiling: shining knights, vanquished monsters, mountains jutting from the earth. It seemed to be a depiction of the creation of the world. There were even crystals embedded into the surface here and there, twinkling like stars.

But based on the content of the painting, there was one absolutely pivotal figure who was not present in the center, where she belonged: Stacia, goddess of creation. That part of the painting was done all in white, leaving a bizarre void that drew attention away from the rest of the work.

After puzzling over that for a bit, Eugeo got up from his hands and feet, then spun around in a panic when something brushed his back.

"...?!"

He gaped. Right behind him was the side of a shockingly large bed. It was circular, like the room itself, and nearly ten mels in diameter. Four golden pillars supported a golden canopy, with several layers of fine purple fabric hanging between them. The bed itself was wrapped in a white sheet of what looked like silk from the eastern empire, which shone softly in the moonlight coming through the window.

And lying in the middle of that bed was a single figure. The sheer hanging fabric blocked the light, revealing nothing but the general silhouette.

Eugeo sucked in a sharp breath and jumped to attention. He'd been here for at least a few minutes, and he hadn't sensed the other person's presence at any point. That was hard enough to believe, but even more difficult was the realization that he'd been sleeping against the side of the bed for hours. How had that happened...?

At last, Eugeo recalled the most recent memory from his vague, jumbled chronology.

That's right...I fought against Commander Bercouli...the hero of yore. I used my sword's Memory Release to freeze us both...and just before both our life numbers ran out, some little man dressed like a clown—Prime Senator Chudelkin? He waltzed in and said some very strange things. Then he crunched the ice roses with his shoes...and...

That was the end of his memories. Perhaps the clownish man had brought him here, but the reason was unclear. Without thinking, he rummaged around his waist, but there was no sword there.

Plagued by a sudden sense of vulnerability, Eugeo squinted at the figure on the bed. Was it friend or foe…? But this was Central Cathedral, and likely the top floor, at that. Nobody he found here would be an ally.

He considered sneaking right out of the room, but his desire to know the identity of the sleeping figure won out. No matter how he stretched, though, he couldn't make out the face behind the hanging fabric.

He held his breath and put his knee on the bed. It sank deep into the white silk, like a layer of powdered snow, and Eugeo had to reach out and prop himself up on his hands. They, too, sank into the smooth fabric.

The memory of that terrible dream and the sensation of its enveloping bed returned to him in a flash, and he shivered. Eugeo put his other leg on the bed and slowly crawled toward the center.

As he crossed the impossibly large bed, Eugeo had to wonder: If the bed beneath him was filled with the finest, softest down, how many feathers would there be in total? When he carefully collected the loose, fallen feathers from the ducks the family kept out back in Rulid, it had taken half a year to make one thin, shabby blanket.

He stopped just before the sheer hanging curtains and listened closely. At the very edge of his hearing was the sound of smooth, regular breathing. The mystery person was still asleep.

Carefully, so carefully, he slipped his right hand under the curtain and lifted it, achingly slowly. When the light of the evening finally landed on the interior portion of the bed, Eugeo's eyes bulged.

It was a woman.

She was dressed in a light-purple nightgown—the same color as a Stacia Window—hemmed with silver thread, with pale and delicate hands folded atop her stomach. Her arms and fingers were as slender as a doll's, but the swelling mounds pushing up the gown were rich and full, and he hastily looked past them without lingering. At the wide-open neck, her skin was smooth and dazzlingly white.

Lastly, he looked at her face. Instantly, he felt as though his soul were being sucked out of his body. He went into tunnel vision, unable to sense anything else.

What incredible perfection. She didn't even seem human.

Alice the Integrity Knight had an unassailable beauty, of course, but hers was still a beauty that existed within the human spectrum. And that was natural—Alice was a human.

But this person sleeping no more than a mel away was...

The finest sculptor in Centoria could spend his entire life in pursuit of total mastery and still be unable to create such beauty. Eugeo couldn't think of the words to describe even a single feature of her face. He would say that she had "lips like flower petals," except that Eugeo did not know of any flowers with such delicate, pristine curves.

The lashes on her closed eyelids and the long flowing hair that spilled over the bed looked like molten silver. It gleamed coldly in the blue darkness and white moonlight.

Like some kind of fly lured by sweet nectar, Eugeo was stunned, unable to think. The only thing filling his empty head was the desire to reach out and touch that hair and cheek, to feel them with his own skin.

He slid forward a bit more on his knees, until a scent like nothing he'd ever smelled before rose into his nostrils. His outstretched fingertips were closer...almost there...on that smooth, flawless skin...

No, Eugeo!
Run!

He felt like a voice had shouted from somewhere in the distance.

There was a burst of sparks inside his head, driving away just a bit of the thick fog clouding his mind. Eugeo's eyes blinked and bulged, and he abruptly drew his hand back.

Why did that voice...sound so familiar...? he wondered in a daze, his ability to think slowly returning. *What...happened to me...? What am I doing here...?*

He stared at the woman sleeping before him, trying to reconcile his presence there, and suddenly felt another heavy layer of sleep threatening to engulf him. He tore his eyes away and shook his head in an attempt to fight it off.

Think. I've got to think. I should know who this is. It's a person sleeping alone on an extravagant bed on the top floor of Central Cathedral. In other words, this must be the most powerful figure in the Axiom Church—and the ruler of all the human lands in existence...

It was the church pontifex, Administrator.

Eugeo repeated that name over and over, now that he could remember it. This was the person who stole Alice, took out her memories, and made her into an Integrity Knight. The most powerful caster of sacred arts, whom even the wise and unfathomable Cardinal couldn't defeat. The ultimate enemy of both Eugeo and Kirito.

And here she was, sleeping right before him.

Could I...beat her now?

Without thinking, he reached for his waist with his trembling hand, but he found no sword there. Either Chudelkin had taken it, or it was still at the bottom of the Great Bath, buried under ice. Even asleep, she was too much for Eugeo to handle without a weapon...

Wait.

There was still one. A very small one, but in a sense, a weapon more powerful than any Divine Object.

Eugeo reached up to his chest and pressed down on his shirt. The sensation of a hard cross pushed back into his palm. It was his final ace, Cardinal's secret weapon.

If he stuck this dagger into Administrator's body, Cardinal's special attack arts would cross time and space to burn her alive.

"...!"

But he could only exhale in anguish, the dagger clutched in his hand through his shirt.

The knife was supposed to be for Alice. She wouldn't be killed, of course, merely put to sleep by Cardinal's magic so her memories could be restored, returning her to the original Alice. If he used it on Administrator, that might stop her, but it would hold no meaning to Eugeo. Perhaps there was a way to bring Alice back without the dagger once Administrator was out of the picture, but there was no guarantee of that.

As he hesitated, grappling with a question with no easy answers, he thought he heard that strange voice again.

Eugeo...run...

But before the message from that terribly faint voice could take root in his consciousness—the woman's silver eyelashes twitched.

Eugeo could only gaze on in dull surprise as her pale eyelids slowly opened. He couldn't even move his eyes, much less the hand holding his dagger. The mental acuity he'd fought so hard to regain began to shred apart again.

The woman's lids closed before they had opened all the way, then resumed their upward drift, teasing him. By the third blink, they were entirely open at last.

"Ah..."

Eugeo didn't even register the sound that tumbled out of his mouth. The woman's eyes were a pure silver color he had never seen in any human iris in his life. Around that mirrorlike surface was a pale rainbow shine that wobbled and rippled like water. They gleamed with such a beautiful richness that every gem in the world paled in comparison.

He was petrified like a statue, kneeling atop the bed, as the woman slowly rose to a sitting position in a way that suggested no weight at all; her upper half hovered up as if pulled by some invisible force, while her hands stayed folded over her stomach. That long silver hair hung down her back in one solid flow, trailing with a breeze that wasn't there.

With her eyes opened, the woman (or girl—she looked younger now that her eyes were open) lifted a hand to her mouth and yawned slightly, without a single acknowledgment of Eugeo's presence.

She folded her knees to the right, shifting her center of weight so that she had to prop herself up with her left hand on the cover. It was in that seductive pose that the girl finally turned her head to look straight at Eugeo.

Her flat silver eyes with their rainbow-colored edges didn't look like they belonged to any human being—there were no pupils. Despite their beauty, they reflected all the light like mirrors, allowing no glimpse into her emotional center.

He gazed into his dumbfounded reflection in those little mirrors as the girl's pearly lips parted. She spoke in a gorgeous voice, as sweet as honey and pure as crystal.

"You poor child."

It took some time for him to understand what she'd said to him. Without realizing how slow his wits were working, he repeated, "Huh...? Poor...?"

"Yes. Very pitiful."

Her voice had a beguiling quality, a combination of innocent beauty and sultry seductiveness. The gleaming pearl lips curled into a subtle grin, emitting more of that honeyed tone.

"You are like a wilted flower in its little bed. No matter how you extend your roots into the soil, no matter how much you stretch your leaves into the breeze, you cannot touch a single drop of dew."

"Flower…bed…"

His brows knotted as he tried to puzzle out the meaning of her words. The fog shrouding his mind still hung thick, but something in her words brought a stab of pain to his heart.

"You understand. You know just how thirsty and starving you are."

"…For what…?" he heard his own voice say.

She stared at him with those mirror eyes, grin still in place.

"For love."

For…love?
As though…I don't know…what love is…

"Precisely correct. You don't know what it means to be loved, you poor child."

That's not true.

Mom…loved me. When I had a nightmare, when I couldn't sleep…she would hold me and sing me lullabies.

"But did that love truly belong to you, and you alone? It didn't, did it? It was spread among all your siblings, and you just happened to receive it by default…"

That's a lie. Mom loved me…She loved only me…

"You wished she only loved you. But she didn't. So you hated your father, your brothers, for stealing your mother's love."

Liar. I…I don't hate Dad or my brothers.

"Is that true…? But you slashed him."

……
Slashed who…?

*   *   *

"There was that red-haired girl who might've been the first one to love you and only you…and you slashed the man who tried to take her by force. Because you hated him. He stole what would have only been yours."

No…that's not why I swung my sword at Humbert.

"But it didn't satisfy your thirst. Nobody loves you. They all forgot about you. They decided they didn't need you, and they cast you aside."

No…that's not true. I…I wasn't abandoned…
That's wrong…I know it is. I have Alice.

The recollection of that name seemed to clear away some of the thick fog shrouding his mind. Eugeo clenched his eyes shut. A warning voice in the back of his head said he had to do something, had to act.

Before he could do anything, that bewitching voice slid in through his eardrums again.

"Is that really true…? Does she really love only you…?" she said, pity mixed with a bit of mockery. "You're forgetting. So I'll help you remember the true memories you've buried deep in your heart."

Then his vision tilted.

The luxurious down bed vanished, replaced by a deep, dark hole through which he fell without end.

Just then, he smelled fresh grass.

The sunlight was green where it hit the earth through the leaves, and his ears were full of the twittering of birds and the rustling of grass underfoot.

He was running alone through a thick forest.

His point of view was strangely low, his paces short. He looked down and saw skinny little child's legs sticking out from a pair of short trousers. But soon it felt natural again, and the only thing he felt was overwhelming haste and loneliness.

For some reason, he hadn't seen Alice all morning.

Once he finished his morning chores of caring for the cows and pulling weeds in the herb garden, Eugeo raced off for the usual meeting spot: the great old tree outside of town. But no matter how long he waited, Alice did not show up. Neither did his other childhood friend, the black-haired boy.

He waited for them until the sun reached the highest point in the sky, then he trotted off toward Alice's house, filled with a strange sense of unease. She had probably gotten in trouble for some mischief and was forbidden from going to see him. But when he reached her house, Mrs. Zuberg simply shook her head and said, "That's strange. She left quite early this morning. Kiri-boy came along, so I was sure you'd be with them."

Eugeo mumbled his thanks and left the village elder's house, then continued his search, the feeling of unease turning to panic. But Kirito and Alice were nowhere to be found—not in any of their playing spots or hideouts, and certainly not in the center square, where Zink and his sidekicks liked to hang out.

There was only one other place he could think of. That round little clearing deep in the woods to the east, where the other children didn't dare go. It was their secret spot, full of flowers and sweet fruit, a place the adults called the Fairy Ring.

He raced straight there, feeling the sniffles coming. He was urged on by loneliness, suspicion, and the presence of some third, unknown emotion.

When he finished running down the twisted trail and approached their secret clearing around an especially thick old tree, he spotted a golden shine between the trunks and came to a stop.

That was the familiar gleam of Alice's golden hair. For some reason, he held his breath and listened. Traces of murmured words reached his ears on the wind.

Why...? Why? he repeated to himself as he snuck up to the

clearing. Self-pity and misery threatened to crush him as he hid behind the mossy trunk and peered into the clearing, which was overflowing with Solus's light.

Alice sat in the middle of the profusion of colorful flowers with her back to him. He couldn't see her face, but the long golden hair, blue dress, and white apron couldn't belong to anyone else.

Next to her was a head of spiky, coarse black hair. His best friend in the world, Kirito.

Cold, clinging sweat flooded his palms.

Kirito's voice traveled to the edge of the clearing, nonchalant. "Hey...we should head back soon, or we'll get busted."

Alice replied, "We're still fine. Let's stay a little longer...Just a bit?"

Oh no.

I don't want to be here.

But Eugeo's feet might as well have been tree roots stuck into the ground.

He couldn't tear his eyes away from the sight of Alice's head leaning closer to Kirito's.

Little shreds of whispering.

It was like a painting, two small figures leaning together in the bright sun, surrounded by brilliant flowers.

No, no, no.

This is a lie. It's all lies, he shouted from somewhere dark. But no matter how hard he tried to deny it, the certainty that this was some truthful memory summoned from the very depths of his mind grew firmer, filling his chest like bile.

"There...you see?"

She giggled. The forest scene vanished into a smug whisper.

Eugeo was on the massive bed in the middle of the pontifex's chamber atop Central Cathedral, but he couldn't dispel the golden shine from his eyes when he closed his lids. His ears still heard phantom whispers from the two.

His voice of reason claimed he met Kirito two years ago, well after Alice was taken away, but it failed to vanquish the dark feeling that filled his heart. He heaved and panted, eyes bulging, while the silver-haired girl gazed at him with pity.

"Do you understand now...? Even her love does not belong only to you. In fact...one wonders if there was any love for you to begin with."

That sweet voice slid into his mind, each lilted question and insinuation wreaking havoc on his thoughts. Suddenly, boundless hunger and loneliness stood out in stark relief to the rest of his emotions. The surface of his ego cracked and fell away, leaving only the raw desire underneath.

"But I'm not like her, Eugeo."

Her most provocative suggestion yet came gushing into Eugeo's mind with the scent of juicy fruit dipped thick in honey.

"I will love you. I'll give you, and only you, all the love I have."

Through half-clouded eyes, Eugeo saw the beautiful girl with the silver hair and eyes—Administrator, highest power of the Axiom Church—give him a mind-melting smile. She shifted her legs against the soft sheet and straightened her back. Her hands came up to the chest of her purple silk nightgown to play with the ribbon that held it closed. With graceful fingers, she pulled at the silver ribbon, teasing it open ever so slowly. The full white bosoms that peeked out of the wide collar swayed enticingly.

"Come to me, Eugeo."

Her whisper was like the voice of his mother in his dream and also like the murmuring of Alice he'd heard during his vision.

In a daze, Eugeo watched the sheer purple cloth fall away from her frighteningly slim waist like flower petals. She really *was* like a flower—the devilish predatory kind that lured in small birds and insects with its powerful perfume and succulent nectar.

Part of Eugeo was able to recognize the danger as such, but the gravitational pull of that delicate, pale fruit in the midst of the purple petals was so strong, in a mind so frayed by the earlier illusions, that he felt like he was sinking deeper into some sticky liquid.

You've never been loved in a way that truly satisfies you, Administrator had said. Now Eugeo himself was beginning to admit this was true. When he was younger, he really did love his parents, brothers, and friends without reservation. The sight of his mother delighted at the flowers he picked for her, and his father and brothers happily eating the fish he caught, filled young Eugeo with joy. He even went into the forest to find healing herbs when Zink the bully and his friends would get sick.

But what did they do for you? After the love you showed them, what did they do for you?

That. That was the part he couldn't remember.

Again, Administrator's gentle grin twisted, and a scene from his past flooded up to greet him.

It was the spring of his tenth year, the day that all the children in the village were brought to the clearing so that the elder could assign their callings. He watched nervously as Elder Gasfut glanced down at him from the podium and announced a significant surprise: "Carver of the Gigas Cedar."

Still, some of the children around him made envious comments. The carver was a prestigious, hallowed position that had existed since the founding of Rulid, and while he wouldn't get a sword, he'd at least get to swing a real ax. Eugeo wasn't disappointed at the time, by any means.

He raced back home, clutching the parchment roll tied with

a red ribbon, proud to show it off to his family. After the initial silence, it was the middle brother who spoke first. He clicked his tongue and complained that he thought it was going to be the day he didn't have to shovel the cow poop anymore. Then the eldest brother noted that this threw off their plan for the year's planting. His father grunted and asked Eugeo when that job would end and whether he would have time for the fields after he got home. His mother disappeared into the kitchen, wary of their wrath.

In the eight years since, Eugeo's role at home had always been small. And yet, the earnings he made as carver went into Father's care and eventually turned into more sheep and new tools for the farm. Meanwhile, Zink the apprentice man-at-arms got to spend all his salary on himself, feasting on white bread with thick slices of meat and showing off his fancy hobnailed boots and his sword with its smooth leather scabbard. Meanwhile, Eugeo drudged around on his worn-down shoes, with nothing but stale, leftover bread in his lunch sack.

"There, you see? Did the people you loved ever once do anything for you in return? Or did they actually take joy in your misery and mock you instead?"

Yes...that's right.

Two years after Alice was taken away by the Integrity Knight, in his eleventh summer, Eugeo remembered Zink telling him that now that the elder's daughter was gone, there was no girl left in the village who would care for him. The look in his eyes made it clear that he thought Eugeo deserved it. He'd been best friends with Alice, the prettiest and most talented girl in the village, and Zink was delighted at his downfall.

Ultimately, no one in Rulid ever repaid Eugeo's sentiments. He had the right to receive what he offered in a fair exchange, but instead, he was denied that privilege.

*   *   *

"Then what's wrong with giving back some of that misery and frustration you've been feeling? Don't you want to? I bet it would feel good to become an Integrity Knight and fly back to your home in all your glory, riding that silver dragon. You can make all those people who humiliated you crawl around in the dirt so you can step on their heads with your shiny boots. Only then can you finally regain all that's been stolen from you. And that's not all..."

Slowly, flirtatiously, the silver-haired girl removed the arms covering her chest. Without their support, her soft, shapely curves bounced like ripe fruit.

Administrator held out her arms to Eugeo and gave him a luxurious smile. "At last, you can know the joy of being truly loved," she whispered. "It's true fulfillment that numbs you from head to toe. I'm not like those people who only took from you. If you love me, I will give back every bit of love in return. The deeper and more truly you love me, the greater pleasure I will show you, bliss that you could never even imagine."

Every last drop of Eugeo's mental strength was being sucked up by the demonic flower. Only the tiniest last shred of reason remaining deep in his heart tried to fight back.

Is that really...what love is about?
Is it really like money...something with numerical value to be traded...?

He thought he heard a voice cry, *That's not true, Eugeo!*—and he turned to see a red-haired girl in a gray uniform lunging for him out of the darkness. Before he could reach back, many thick black curtains fell between them, leaving only the sadness of the girl's eyes in his mind.

Next it was a different voice from a different direction: *You're wrong, Eugeo. You don't give your love in order to get something in return.*

He spun around in the darkness to catch a glimpse of a field, where he saw a golden-haired girl standing in a blue dress. Her blue eyes shone like the one exit from this bottomless swamp, and Eugeo willed strength into his wilted legs to join her.

Once again, the black curtains fell, erasing the green pasture. Without a guiding light, Eugeo halted in the dark. He could no longer stand that burning thirst. The knowledge that he'd been unfairly abused, taken advantage of, and deprived since childhood turned his self-pity and misery into brine that seared his parched throat.

At last, Eugeo hung his head and began to crawl. Bit by bit, he crept toward the oasis of nectar and its sweet, heady perfume.

His fingers parted the smooth sheet of silk and brushed chilly skin. He looked up, and the silver-haired girl with the beauty of a goddess gave him a transcendent smile and took his hand. She pulled him gently, and he toppled forward without a fight. Her utterly naked body enveloped Eugeo, embracing him in its pliable softness.

At his ear, she whispered sweetly, "Don't you want it, Eugeo? Don't you want to forget all the sad things and just have your way with me? But not yet. I told you—first you have to love me. Just repeat what I tell you. Put your full trust in me and pledge me your everything. We'll start with the initiation of the sacred art."

The only reality for Eugeo by this point was the sweet, soft sensation that surrounded him in every way. Dully, as though it came from someone else, he heard himself croak, "System... Call."

"That's right...Now continue...Remove Core Protection."

For the first time, he sensed her voice faltering and the presence of some kind of emotion.

He mumbled the phrase's first unfamiliar word.

*   *   *

"Remove…"

When he gave up and submitted to her orders, he felt his existence getting lighter and thinner. That hunger and thirst that had plagued him for so very, very long melted and vanished into the sweet nectar. But so, too, did some very important feelings he'd held deep inside his heart.

Was this really…the best idea…?

The tiny little spark of doubt flamed up in his hollowing insides, but the next word was already tumbling out of his lips before he could answer his own question.

"Core…"

I'm just tired of being sad. Tired of being in pain.

There was no guarantee of love here. He would not find the love he was promised. And even…even if Alice regained her memory, would she even care about him? Would she want the man who'd violated the Taboo Index to attack Humbert and had fought against many Integrity Knights in open rebellion against the Church? Or would she fear and despise him…?

He would rather stop right here than have to face that outcome.

Through the haze, Eugeo could vaguely sense that if he said the third word, his two-year journey would come to an irreversible end. But if doing so could allow him to forget his sad, painful past—and he could soak in this silver-haired girl's love—a part of him was fine with that.

"That's it…now come, Eugeo. Come into me," she whispered into his ear, the sweetest and most delectable of sounds. "Welcome to eternal stasis…"

As he said the third and final word, a tear fell down Eugeo's cheek.

3

"There...we...goooo!"

For the umpteenth time, I hauled myself up, caught my right leg on the corner of the marble, and swung up onto a flat surface at last.

My joints and muscles, taxed well beyond their limit, screamed and throbbed like they were being seared by flames. Large beads of sweat rolled down my forehead and neck, but I couldn't even move my hands to wipe them away; I couldn't do anything other than pant. The fatigue was so real and all-encompassing that it was hard to remind myself that this was just the STL's virtual world.

Once the moon had fully risen, we spent the next two hours in another agonizing climb, and now that I was finally up on the ninety-fifth floor of Central Cathedral, I didn't even have the energy to look around. I let my limbs lie flat, closed my eyes, and waited for my life value to return.

There were nearly fifteen floors between the terrace with all the stone minions and here. It wouldn't have been that bad if not for the golden knight fixed to my back by her slender chain, necessitating all that time and stamina.

Alice Synthesis Thirty had impressively overcome the Seal of the Right Eye, that mysterious system that kept all Underworldians in check, but the cost had been severe. It had exploded her jasper-like right eye without a trace, and the shock and pain had knocked her unconscious.

The Underworldians' souls were stored in lightcubes, an artificial memory medium. Perhaps because of that, they had a tendency to be more susceptible to psychological shock. When they were faced with immense sadness, fear, or anger, they went into a kind of temporary shutdown to protect their fluctlights from some kind of fatal error—but in a world without the concept of crime, it was quite rare for such extreme emotions to manifest. It had happened to Alice's sister, Selka, two years ago, too, when we were attacked by the goblins in the northern cave.

Alice went unconscious merely to soften the shock of breaking through that eye seal. I expected she would awaken eventually; if there had been some fatal-error damage to her fluctlight, she would have died on the spot, as Raios Antinous had.

In that sense, it was remarkable that Eugeo, who had suffered the same phenomenon as Alice, stayed awake and finished his swing when it happened. He'd been fully spent after we got tossed into the cells, but he still responded when I spoke to him.

So the reason for the Underworldians' mental fragility and absolute obedience to orders was still a mystery, but at least I knew it was possible for them to overcome it; Eugeo and Alice proved that. Yes, they were technically artificial intelligences, but the power contained in their souls was no different from that of people in the real world...

These thoughts and more went through my head for an hour on the terrace with the minions while I waited for Alice to recover, but she never opened her eyes. I used sacred arts to stop the bleeding, but I had neither the resources nor the skill to heal her entirely. While I waited, the moon rose and granted some spatial resources, but I needed them to generate the ice picks for climbing. The best I could do was rip the hem of my shirt to make an impromptu bandage for her, then continue climbing the tower with the unconscious knight weighing me down.

I removed the chain that connected us, tried hauling Alice's slender but unbelievably heavy body over my back, and seriously considered removing the golden armor and Osmanthus Blade that made up most of that weight. However, it would have been stupid to leave those tools of hers behind now that she had made up her mind to fight on our side.

Instead, I steeled myself, hooked the chain to the knight's body, and began climbing up toward the top of Central Cathedral in the distant night sky. After two hours of miserable effort, the sight of a new terrace brought me such relief, I accidentally dropped one of the hooks. All I could do was hope nobody was waiting on the ground far below, unsuspecting.

At any rate, once I had made it the ninety yards straight up that vertical wall to the ninety-fifth floor, I figured I had earned the right to lie down on flat ground for a little while. I wasn't planning to move for another three minutes at least.

Just when I hoped to enjoy the feeling of every muscle in my body relaxing, I was interrupted by a quiet groaning from atop my back.

"Mm...muhhh...," the knight said, her breath tickling my neck. "Where...? What...did I...?"

She tried to get up, but the chain quickly went taut, and the weight returned to my back.

"These chains...Kirito...Did you carry me...up here...?"

That's right—you owe me some gratitude, I thought.

"Oh no, you're all sweaty! You'll stain my uniform! Get away from me!" she shouted, whacking the back of my head. My forehead smacked the hard marble floor.

"I don't know...what I did to deserve that shabby treatment...," I grumbled as I undid the chain and removed the cargo from my back, then leaned against a nearby pillar. The knight didn't utter a word of thanks for my extreme physical labor; she was busy flapping her white skirt in an attempt to air it out. Once she finished, she felt the sleeve that had been pressed to the back of my neck the entire climb and glared at it suspiciously. Well, I wasn't going to let this insult go without some banter of my own.

"If you're that concerned, why don't you go and take a bath, princess?" I said sarcastically, but fastidious Alice actually looked like she was taking the question seriously. "I'm just kidding!" I added. "There's no way we're going back down all that way."

"That won't be necessary, actually. There's a Great Bath for the knights just five floors below us."

"Wha…?"

Now it was my turn to look baffled. After escaping the underground prison, running through battle after battle, and completing this unplanned wall-climbing campaign, I would be lying if I said I didn't want the chance to wash off the dust and sweat. It didn't even have to be a bath, just a water pump—and then I looked around at last.

Like the name Morning Star Lookout suggested, the ninety-fifth floor was built to be one giant observation deck. The four edges of the tower had no walls here—which was why I was climbing up to it—just round pillars supporting the ceiling at ten-foot intervals. Given how open it was, I could now understand why Administrator placed those minion gargoyles along the walls below.

We were on the outermost part of the floor, which was a terrace with the occasional little set of stairs leading within. The interior was slightly elevated, with marble sculptures, verdant plants, and tastefully designed tables and chairs. I had no doubt that the wide-open view of the Underworld below would be breathtaking in daytime.

On the north end, a great set of stairs led to the adjacent floors. We were the only people in sight.

But had Eugeo passed through here yet or not?

Seven hours had passed since I was separated from him on the eightieth floor. I had to scramble for my life up a sheer wall and he had regular old stairs to use, so he should have gotten here much quicker.

But the problem was that he had to face a foe much stronger than the minions: Bercouli Synthesis One, commander of the Integrity Knights, a hero of legend stronger than Vice Commander

Fanatio and Alice, both of whom had already fought me off without much trouble.

Eugeo was mighty, too, of course. In terms of sword skill, he had probably surpassed me already. But skill alone could not dispatch the superhuman Integrity Knights, especially the senior ones. It required taking advantage of the opponent's mindset and utilizing anything you possibly could in the vicinity—a true "anything-goes" approach. Could earnest, straightforward Eugeo pull that off...?

Alice finished her own examination of the vicinity. "I say this with no relation to the issue of baths...but I must doubt that your friend Eugeo has come up this far yet."

"Huh? Why?"

"Because once we were thrown out of the cathedral, this floor became the only place we could get back inside. It's really obvious from a glance...so if he had gotten here already, he would likely be waiting for you."

"...I see. You've got a point," I said, crossing my arms. If Eugeo had reached this floor before us, he'd have been either caught or killed by now. While I'd been doubting him just a moment ago, I also wanted to believe Eugeo was good enough not to end up with either of those fates.

"The other thing for Eugeo," Alice said, clearly not realizing how naturally that name slipped out of her mouth, "is that if he came up the stairs from the Cloudtop Garden, he would run across our most powerful fighter before reaching the Morning Star Lookout. That would be Uncle...Commander Bercouli."

Setting aside the use of the word *uncle*, I couldn't help but be curious about something she said.

"Is he really that tough? This knights' commander guy."

Alice turned to me with a grin, part of her face still hidden by the makeshift bandage. "I have never once bested him in a practice duel. If you lost to me, and Eugeo is at your level, then by that logic, he will not win, either."

"...Sure, by that logic. But if not for what happened, I may not have actually lost to you, either," I grumbled.

The golden knight ignored me and continued, "Uncle's skill with the blade is absolutely first-class, but his Perfect Weapon Control is simply divine. His Time-Splitting Sword, like the name suggests, is capable of piercing time itself. I suppose you would understand if I said that when he cuts the air, that slicing force remains suspended there for a time. Even if you avoid his strikes, eventually you will be trapped in a cage of blades that you cannot see. The slightest move might cost you a hand or a foot or, worse, your head—but if you don't move, you are an easy target. Ultimately, any opponent of Uncle's will be forced to stand in place and succumb to one of his greatest attacks like a practice dummy."

"...The slices...remain suspended..."

It was hard to imagine from the way she described it, but it sounded like the chronological length of a swing was extended out into the future. If so, it was a frightful power indeed. It would totally override the strength of the Aincrad style, which was to reduce the strength of any single blow but make up for it by extending the range and time of our attacks with combos.

What would have happened to Eugeo against such a foe? I was certain he wouldn't be dead, but a chilling foreboding crept up my spine. Perhaps we *ought* to head down in search of my partner after all. But what if he'd already been captured and taken to Administrator's chamber on the top floor? What if she was performing some dangerous sacred arts on him, with her knowledge of all the user commands...?

At last, the fatigue was starting to leave my legs, and I got to my feet, if unsteadily. I glared at the stairs on the north end of the floor and bit my lip. What I would give for a sacred art that could tell me Eugeo's current location—but as a basic rule, no art could be cast on a human target that wasn't present. If that were not the case, Administrator and Cardinal's duel would have been over ages ago. But if the target were an object rather than a person, there were other options...

Only then did I realize that there was such an easy way to solve this problem.

"Of course…that's right."

I motioned to Alice, who was looking at me with suspicion, raised my right hand, and at a moderate volume announced, "System Call!"

My fingers glowed purple, a sign that the spatial resources were charged again after the exhausting climb up the wall. Careful to control my emotions, I enunciated the following commands: "Generate Umbra Element. Adhere Position. Object ID, DLSS703. Discharge."

It was always good to memorize your vocabulary. Naturally, my search target was the unique ID of Eugeo's Blue Rose Sword. From what I was able to guess, DLSS was probably an abbreviation for "Double-Edged Longsword Single-Hand," while the string of numbers was the identification for that particular sword within that category. My black sword's ID was DLSS102382, which suggested that when the Blue Rose Sword was generated in the early days of the Underworld, there were only about seven hundred one-handed longswords at the time, but by the time my sword was crafted just two years ago, there were over a hundred thousand. At least, if my deduction was correct…

The little darkness element floated steadily downward until it landed on the ground a short distance away and burst.

"…It's below."

"So it would seem," Alice noted with mild interest.

I clutched and released my fist a few times, sensing that some of my fatigued life was back, but I knew that Alice had suffered more damage. I glanced her way and asked, "Do you think you can heal your eye…?"

She put her fingers to the strip of cloth that had previously been part of my shirt and asked, "Did…you do this?"

"Yeah…It managed to stop the bleeding, but that was the best I could do with my sacred arts. I thought maybe you…"

"Of course. My sacred arts authority is far beyond yours," she snipped in her usual manner. Her visible eye turned to the sky to stare at the full moon. "But there is not enough sacred power in the air to generate the light elements needed to restore my lost eye. It will not be possible until Solus rises."

"Then perhaps if you converted one of your high-priority obj—I mean, one of your precious valuables into power…Your armor, perhaps…"

"Even the art to return a receptacle into its basic sacred power requires more than a small amount of power to begin with. Didn't you learn that at the academy?" she said with exasperation, then thought it over. "I do still feel the pain, and my vision on the right side is limited, but neither is enough to prevent me from fighting. I shall be able to continue in this state for now."

"B-but…"

"More importantly, I want to feel. I want to feel the evidence of my intention to fight against the Axiom Church I've believed in for so long…"

In that sense, I couldn't argue. This fight was as much about Alice creating her own destiny as it was about mine.

"All right…if it comes to combat, I'll protect your right," I said, eyeing the main staircase. "We've got to hurry, though. Based on the movement of that darkness element, Eugeo's got to be pretty far down from here."

Technically, my search spell was for the location of Eugeo's sword, not Eugeo, but he wouldn't let go of it unless something very bad happened.

Alice looked to the stairs as well and announced, "I'll take the lead—I know the way. Then again…we're only going down the stairs." And without allowing me any chance to interject, she strode toward them, boots clicking. I hurried to keep up.

Cool air flowed up from the descending stairs at the north end of the floor, and I couldn't sense anyone in the darkness below. Even on the lower floors, there was very little sense of activity; up here at the top, Central Cathedral was simply cold and dead, like a series of lavish, beautiful ruins. It was hard to think of this as the center of power for the organization that oversaw the entire human world.

There was supposedly a senate in addition to the Integrity Knighthood among the upper echelon of the Axiom Church. It seemed strange that I'd ascended so high in the tower yet had not seen a single one.

I caught up to Alice on the right side as she descended and voiced my suspicions. The knight looked a bit perplexed, then whispered back, "As a matter of fact, even we knights aren't told anything about the senators. I've heard that the ninety-sixth floor and up is a section called the senate, but we are forbidden to enter..."

"Oh...So what do the senators actually do, anyway?"

"...The Taboo Index," she said, her voice even quieter now. "The purpose of the senate is to observe and confirm that all people are following the Taboo Index. When there is an Index violation, they dispatch an Integrity Knight to control the situation. I went to take in you and Eugeo from North Centoria Imperial Swordcraft Academy two days ago on just such an order."

"...I see...So the senate is kind of like a proxy for the pontifex. I'm surprised that Administrator would give them such powerful privileges, knowing how cautious she is. Unless the senators have their memories controlled the same way the knights do..."

Alice scowled and shook her head. "Please don't talk about memory. I don't want my remaining good eye to start hurting, too."

"S-sorry. I think you're safe now, though...Eugeo's eye seal broke, too, and nothing much happened to him after that..."

"...Let's hope you're right," she said, rubbing her eye patch.

I recalled what had happened on that exterior terrace. Alice had been shaken a number of times before she ultimately swore to fight against the Axiom Church and its leader, but at no point did her Piety Module ever show signs of activity. I assumed that the memory fragment Administrator took from Alice had to do with her sister, Selka, or childhood friend Eugeo, but unlike what had happened with Eldrie, when Eugeo mentioned Selka's name to her at the academy, no purple prism appeared from her forehead.

So what in the world was the memory that Administrator took from Alice's mind?

It was rather pointless to wonder about that now. Once Cardinal performed her Reverse Synthesis Ritual (if you could call it that), Alice would regain her past memory, and the Integrity Knight I was with now would cease to be...

Again, I sensed a subtle little twinge in my chest as I mechanically walked on.

The only sounds on the late-night staircase were two echoing pairs of feet. After five repetitions of landings with bright-red carpets, the descending stairs came to an end, revealing a very large set of doors. We'd passed the ninety-fourth through ninety-first floors, and there were no marks of battle anywhere.

Alice came to a stop, and I sent her a questioning glance.

"Yes...this is it. The Great Bath on the ninetieth floor. I would assume that Uncle wouldn't choose such a place as his defense point...but then again, knowing him..." She trailed off as she put her hand to the door. Just a light push, and the thick slab of marble rotated without a sound. Instantly a wave of thick white mist pushed out, and I turned away on instinct.

"Whoa...that's some major steam. How big is this bath? I can't even see inside."

Although it obviously wasn't the time, it was very tempting to strip off my sweaty clothes and jump into that hot cleansing water. Only when I took a step inside the cloudy air did I realize it was not hot steam but freezing mist.

Alice wasn't expecting this, either—she sneezed daintily, and I promptly unleashed a percussive blast of my own. The veil of white air hovering in front of me gave way, but not because of the force of my sneeze. When I saw the state of the bathing chamber, I stood still in shock.

It had to take up the entire floor of the tower, because the far wall was foggy in the distance. Almost the entire chamber was a bathtub, split in two around a long straight walkway right in front of us. Each bathtub was practically a fifty-meter Olympic pool on its own.

But the truly shocking detail was that the bath-pool on our left was completely frozen white. Even the animal-head faucet in the corner of the bath, pouring water in, was frozen into a curved pillar of ice, indicating that the freezing process had happened in an instant. That would be not a natural effect but the work of sacred arts, of course.

Whatever froze this much water at once was no laughing matter. You'd need at least ten expert casters utilizing ordinary sacred arts with ice elements to achieve this effect.

I headed to the left and descended the stepped lip of the tub so I could rest my foot on the surface of the hard ice. It didn't creak, even with my full weight and heavy sword resting on it. I guessed that the water was frozen all the way to the bottom of the baths.

"Who did this...and why?" I wondered. After a few steps over the wispy surface, my boot landed on something hard. It crumbled delicately. Upon closer examination, I saw a number of the small round objects on the surface of the ice. I reached down and broke one off, then lifted it up.

It was a rose of ice, with many layers of blue, translucent petals.

"...!!"

I'd seen these before on multiple occasions. In the Great Hall of Ghostly Light on the fiftieth floor, when we fought Vice Commander Fanatio Synthesis Two; and in the Cloudtop Garden on the eightieth floor, when we fought Alice Synthesis Thirty. Eugeo utilized his Perfect Weapon Control to immobilize his targets in those situations, producing ice roses just like these.

It wasn't sacred arts that froze this mammoth bathtub solid...

"...It was Eugeo..."

Alice lowered herself on the ice next to me. Her working eye was wide as she gasped, "By the Three...You're saying Eugeo did this...?"

"Yep, no doubt about it. It's the Perfect Control effect of his Blue Rose Sword. But I'll be honest...I didn't think it had this much potential..."

Eugeo claimed his Perfect Weapon Control was designed for slowing down opponents. He was dead wrong—anyone trapped in this hell of ice would lose their life before long.

Perhaps he really did defeat the legendary hero Bercouli. I looked around, desperate for information. The darkness element had indicated that the Blue Rose Sword would be around here, and that meant Eugeo was here, too.

Just then, I heard Alice gasp.

"...!"

I sucked in a sharp breath, too. About twenty yards away was a rather large silhouette. It was unmistakably a human head and shoulder. Someone buried in the ice.

Alice and I shared a glance, then we raced over, scattering ice roses.

I soon realized the person trapped in the ice was not Eugeo. His shoulders and neck were at least twice as thick as my partner's.

I slowed down out of disappointment and caution, but Alice only went faster. "Uncle!" she cried, racing for the frozen silhouette.

That's Commander Bercouli?! Then where's Eugeo...?!

Confused, I increased my speed again. When I caught up several steps later, Alice was on her knees before the burly man, clenching her fists and screaming, "Uncle...! Commander! What happened to you?!"

Alice had seen Eugeo's ice power on the eightieth floor, so she should have understood what the Blue Rose Sword's effect was; when I got closer, I realized what she meant.

The man wasn't simply frozen up to his chest. His rippling, muscular shoulders, trunk-thick neck, and fierce, proud features were all colored in a drab, inorganic gray.

"That's...not part of Eugeo's...Perfect Control effect...," I murmured, stunned.

Her back to me, Alice said, "I...I agree with you. Long ago, Uncle told me...the prime senator has the authority to turn all human beings into stone...even Integrity Knights. I believe the name of the ability is...Deep Freeze."

"Deep...Freeze," I repeated. "Then this old guy—er, I mean, the commander—got turned this way by the prime senator? Aren't they on the same side? Why…? I mean, he should be a valuable force in fighting off intruders, right?"

"I think Uncle secretly questioned the senate orders handed down to him…but like I did, he believed peace was impossible without the rule of the Axiom Church, and he spent countless days battling for that purpose. No matter what powers the prime senator has, there is no call…no reason for him to do such a horrid thing!!"

Tears dropped onto Alice's knees from her left eye. She reached out, not bothering to wipe her cheeks, and clung to the petrified Bercouli. One of the teardrops landed on the commander's forehead and vanished into little sparkles of light.

A sharp crack split the scene.

Alice leaped up to her feet, staring at Bercouli's neck. There was actually a small split there, as though the mild warmth of her tear had melted the stone effect. The fissure widened and grew, throwing off tiny shards of material.

We watched in amazement as the gray statue continued splitting, very gradually changing the angle of its neck. Soon the face was pointing toward us, and the stone around the mouth began to crack. Shards of stone that would have been flesh and blood just hours ago continued to fall away.

Based on the name Deep Freeze, I assumed the command would completely pause an Underworldian's state, body as well as mind. It wouldn't be like spreading liquid plaster over someone in the real world. Through the orders of Stacia, the god of all, his every movement was forbidden—and he was trying to overcome it through willpower alone.

"Uncle…stop, stop it! You'll tear your body apart, Uncle!!" Alice pleaded tearfully. But not for an instant did Commander Bercouli stop his defiance of the gods. With an especially loud crunch, he lifted his eyelids. The eyes revealed were as gray as his skin, but the irises rippled like the surface of water, and they began to regain a very faint bluish color. The absolute strength of will they exuded was so overwhelming, it gave me goose bumps.

He grinned, throwing off another shower of shards, and opened his mouth to emit a hideously raspy but powerful voice.

"...Hey...little Alice. You shouldn't cry...that hard. It ruins... your pretty face."

"Uncle...!!"

"Don't...worry...A single art isn't going to kill a guy like me. Besides..."

Bercouli paused, taking in Alice's tear-streaked face and the impromptu bandage that covered the right side. He gave her a smile full of fatherly love and said, "Oh, I see...little Alice, you made it over that wall...You broke through...the right eye...like I never could...in three centuries..."

"U-Uncle...I...I'm..."

"Don't look at me...that way...I'm...happy for you...Now there's...nothing left...for me to...teach you..."

"That's...that's not true! There are so, so many things...I still want to learn from you, Uncle!!" she cried, not even trying to hide her childish sobs, flinging her arms around his neck.

"You can do it, little Alice," Bercouli whispered into her ear, beatific smile on his lips. "You can...correct the mistakes of the Church...and help guide this world...to its proper...state..."

I could tell that the strength was rapidly draining from his voice. The remarkable willpower coming from the knights' commander's fluctlight was reaching its end at last. His eyes suddenly turned to me; they were losing their focus and turning gray again. He worked stiffening lips and croaked, "Hey...kid...Take care of...little...Alice..."

"...You bet," I said simply, and the hero of old nodded back, creating a fresh crack in his stony neck. What I interpreted as his final words emerged as white, frosty mist. "Prime Senator Chudelkin...took your...partner 'way...I bet it was...to 'ministrator's...chamber...Better hurry...before he gets trapped in the labyrinth...of his memories..."

And with that, Bercouli the Integrity Knight Commander returned to silent stone. There was something truly appropriate

about the heroic figure he struck, buried to his chest in solid ice, neck and face covered in fine, tiny cracks.

"...Uncle...," Alice whimpered, still clinging to his shoulder. I turned away, considering what the man's words meant.

This Prime Senator Chudelkin was the one who'd placed the Deep Freeze command on Bercouli and taken Eugeo away. That much was certain, because, in a spot not far from the frozen Bercouli, there was a square shaft carved out of the ice all the way down to the floor, as though cut by an electric saw. Eugeo must have used his ice roses' power expecting to go down and take the commander with him, but then the prime senator came along, cut him entirely out of the ice, and took him up to Administrator's chamber at the top of the tower.

I had to wonder what this "labyrinth of memories" meant, though. I didn't like to think about Eugeo being handily brainwashed, but I also had no idea what sort of methods Administrator would use to manipulate his fluctlight directly.

I peered down the square hole and saw, just through the perfectly smooth sides, something shining. I crouched down to see a longsword plunged into the floor of the bath. Even through several inches of ice, I would never mistake that beautiful curve. It was the Blue Rose Sword.

That striking weapon was practically a part of Eugeo; the sight of it left behind under thick ice only made me more worried. I glanced back at Alice, who was still clinging to Bercouli, then drew my black sword and stuck the tip into the ice directly above the Blue Rose Sword. For just an instant, I pushed down.

The ice cracked, split vertically, and crumbled into the shaft nearby. I knelt and squeezed the exposed handle of the Blue Rose Sword, then pulled, wincing against the sensation of well-below-zero-degrees metal on my skin. It resisted a bit, then slid out silently, scattering ice fragments.

I stood up, black sword in my right hand and Blue Rose Sword in my left, and felt my joints buckle with the extra weight. No wonder, since I was holding two very high-priority Divine

Objects, but I wasn't going to complain. Ronie and Tiese, our trainee pages, had worked their palms bloody carrying these swords to Eugeo and me before we were taken to the cathedral.

Now it was my turn to take this sword to Eugeo.

A familiar white leather sheath was on the frosted ice surface nearby. With my sword at my side, I picked up the sheath and placed Eugeo's sword in it. After a little more thought, I then attached the second sheath to my belt on the right side, balancing the weight so I could still move reasonably well.

I exhaled and turned around to find Alice up on her feet. She rubbed the moisture on her cheek with her sleeve and, to hide her embarrassment, grumbled, "The only person mad enough to carry two swords would be some peacock of an elite noble...but oddly enough, it seems to suit you."

"Hmm? Oh..."

I couldn't help but grimace. During *SAO*, my lifeline as a solo player was my flashy Dual Blades style, but I'd hidden that skill for so long, I still felt anxious about showing off a two-sword approach in front of others.

Or maybe that wasn't entirely it. Perhaps I was somehow afraid—even sick—of the ostentatious description of Dual-Bladed Kirito, the hero who'd beaten the Game of Death. I never wanted to take on that particular role again, no matter what anyone said about me.

"...Yeah, but I can't actually swing two swords at once," I told her with a shrug.

Alice nodded as if this were obvious. "If you swing two swords, there is no way to execute a proper ultimate technique. In that sense alone, there is little reason to ever wield two swords at once. Anyway, if the sword is still here, then we ought to assume that the pontifex has apprehended Eugeo already. We ought to hurry; she is not bound by typical logic..."

"Have you...spoken with Administrator before?"

"Only once," she answered, lips pursed. "It was six years ago, after I woke up as an apprentice Integrity Knight with no memory, facing my summoner, and God's proxy in the mortal world, the church pontifex. She was very beautiful and fragile, not the kind of person who has ever held a sword...but her *eyes*..."

She clutched her own shoulders. "Her eyes were silver and reflective, like a mirror...I didn't realize it at the time, but now I do: I was terrified of her. It was an absolute kind of fear, the sort that told me I should never defy her or doubt a word she said, and instead I should offer her my everything."

"Alice...," I murmured, feeling momentary disquiet.

But she sensed what I was thinking, took a deep breath, and raised her head to look at me. "I am fine. I've made up my mind. For the sake of my sister living in the far north...for my unfamiliar family, and for all the citizens of the realm, I must do what I believe is right. Uncle knew about the eye seal that we all bear. That tells me that Bercouli Synthesis One, leader of the Integrity Knights, did not blindly believe that the Axiom Church's reign was entirely good. Our trek down here to get your partner was a failure, but I'm glad that I saw Uncle...I know that my heart is firm and in the right place now."

She crouched and caressed Bercouli's stone cheek, lingering no more than an instant before she turned away, striding purposefully over the ice in the direction we had come. "Let's hurry. We may need to battle the prime senator before we have a chance to face the pontifex herself."

"W-wait...are we just going to leave the commander like that?" I asked, trotting to catch up.

Alice glared at me with her good eye and snapped, "Either we will truss up Prime Senator Chudelkin to make him undo the sacred art...or we will cut him in two and solve the matter that way."

As I struggled to walk with the weight of two swords, I realized I never wanted to make an enemy of this knight again.

We raced back up the five flights of stairs, dealing with extra gravity this time, and stopped when we made it back to the

Morning Star Lookout. I was wheezing with the effort of lugging the Blue Rose Sword, but the Integrity Knight was largely unaffected, despite wearing so much armor that her weight couldn't be far from mine. With her frosty-blue eye and snow-white skin, she faced the next staircase with determination.

"Listen to me as you catch your breath. The senators are not much more than simple civilians when it comes to using weapons in short-range combat, but their sacred arts authority is higher than ours. Even in this resource-scarce environment, they can use the catalyst crystals from the Rose Garden to unleash practically unlimited long-range attacks."

"Enemies like that…you need to…sneak up, then stick close," I wheezed between breaths.

"We can't be bothered with personal dignity now," Alice agreed. "If we can successfully approach without detection, that would be best, but there is no guarantee of that. If that plan fails, I will use my sword's Perfect Control to block their sacred arts, and then you can charge them."

"So I'm the suicide-charge guy…," I lamented, recalling how much I hated dealing with mage-type enemies.

Alice arched her eyebrow and offered sarcastically, "We can switch roles, if you prefer. But you will be in charge of blocking their sacred arts."

"Fine, fine, I'll do it."

My black sword was still recovering its life value, and I wasn't sure whether it had enough for a good Perfect Control use. If possible, I preferred to save that for a fight against the pontifex. My sword's ultimate power was a fairly simple one—summoning a giant spear of darkness—that excelled in power, but it didn't have the varied effects Alice's flower storm did.

"If I feel like it, I might favor you with a recovery art from behind," Alice said generously. "You may cause as much damage as you wish, but make sure that Prime Senator Chudelkin survives. If my memory is accurate, he will look like a small man in bright-red-and-blue clown clothes."

"...That...does not sound very...dignified."

"But you must not underestimate him on account of it. In addition to his powerful Deep Freeze ability, he has a number of speedy and powerful arts. He is likely the most powerful caster in the Church, after the pontifex."

"Yeah, I get it. It's pretty much a quest cliché that the little silly-looking guys end up being the toughest enemies."

Alice briefly shot me a suspicious look, then turned her face to the staircase and announced, "Let's go."

We raced up the flight of steps as fast and quiet as we could, and we came upon a cramped and dark hallway, which ended at a black door. The hall was maybe five feet across and lit by eerie green lamps. It was just tight enough to force you to move out of the way if someone was coming from the other direction. The door at the end of the hall was small, too. Alice and I could just walk through without bumping our heads, but a man as large as Bercouli would have to crouch down quite a bit.

It just didn't sit right with me. Normally when you got into the ultimate enemy's stronghold—the final dungeon, if you will—the design and furnishings got fancier and more imposing. And just one floor below, the Morning Star Lookout had been extravagantly outfitted. So why would it suddenly get so cramped and unpleasant, right before the very end?

"Is this...the senate you mentioned earlier...?" I murmured.

"It should be," she replied uncertainly. "It will be clear when we go in, at least."

She strode down the hallway, flicking her golden hair aside to blow the hesitation away. I was starting to think this might be a trap and was tempted to reach out and stop her. But then I thought better of it; the Axiom Church wouldn't set up a trap for intruders this high in the tower. And even if they did, it would be a bold projection of its power, like those minion statues on the walls outside.

The twenty-yard-long hallway did nothing to block our way. In moments, we reached the little door and shared a glance. As the up-close attacker, I grabbed the tiny doorknob to take the lead. It clicked open, no lock, and smoothly swung outward.

There was a sudden gust of cold air from the darkness within, suggesting the thick presence of something. It was the kind of foreboding sensation I got when opening the door to a labyrinth boss chamber in Aincrad—and it made my spine crawl.

I wasn't going to beg Alice to take the lead, of course. I pulled the door all the way open, ducked my head, and looked inside. The hallway continued a short way through, then turned into what looked like an open space with hardly any light. All I could see was a faint, flickering purple light, though the source was unclear.

The moment I moved through the doorway, I heard what sounded like mumbled chanting. I stopped to listen harder: It wasn't just one voice. There were several, perhaps dozens, all in unison. Behind me, Alice murmured that it was sacred arts, and I realized she was right.

I tensed, preparing for multiple attacks all at once, then realized I was mistaken. From what I could hear of the spell words, none included the "generate" command that was a virtual requisite of any attack art.

If I was curious, Alice was downright proactive. "Let's go in. If the senators are preparing some major unrelated sacred art, that suits our purposes. We can sneak through the darkness and get within sword range before they realize it."

"...Oh, good thinking. I'll go first, like we said. Watch my back," I whispered, quietly drawing my black sword. The Blue Rose Sword was only likely to weigh me down in combat, but I wasn't going to just leave it on the ground there. Once Alice had her Osmanthus Blade drawn as well, I resumed sneaking forward.

The closer we got to the dim chamber, the more I noticed a nasty smell in the cold air. It wasn't a fetid odor like animals or blood, but more like the stink of rotting food. I tried to ignore it as I pressed my back to the wall of the corridor and peered into the dark space that I assumed was the senate.

It was large—but more than that, it was *tall*.

At its base, the chamber was a circle about twenty yards across. The curved walls stretched up about three floors to a ceiling hidden in darkness. The structure of it reminded me of Cardinal's Great Library.

There were no lamps in the room, only a flickering purple light coming from the walls here and there. There was also a series of many round objects placed at set intervals, but I couldn't tell what they were.

Then a new light source appeared very close to us. It was a square board glowing light purple—a Stacia Window. And the sphere within it was...

A human head.

Did that mean every last round object here in the cylindrical chamber was...

"...A...h-head...?" I gasped.

"No, they seem to have bodies," Alice noted, as quietly as she could. "But it's like they're growing out of the walls..."

I squinted as best I could. There were indeed necks and shoulders beneath the spheres, but that was all I could make out—their bodies were stuffed right into square boxes mounted into the walls.

Based on the small size of the boxes, I had to assume their limbs were folded into an absolutely minimal space. It didn't look comfortable in the least, but I couldn't actually tell how the people in the boxes felt about it, because their faces showed zero emotion.

Their pale, exposed heads had no traces of hair on their scalps, chins, or brows, and their beady, glassy eyes gazed at nothing but the Stacia Windows right before them. There were complex strings of letters appearing on the windows, at the end of which the box-people would intone, "System Call...Display Rebelling Index" with washed-out, bloodless lips.

I froze. Their voices didn't sound like they belonged to living people. "Are...are these the ones who...?!"

"You're familiar with them?!" Alice snapped. I glanced at her and nodded.

"Yeah...There was this window that opened in the corner of the room right after we had that big fight at Swordcraft Academy two days ago. There was a white face watching me and Eugeo from it...and no doubt about it, it was one of these..."

Alice paused to listen to the box-people chant, then frowned. "The sacred art they are reciting is completely unfamiliar to me...but it seems they have the realm divided into sections. I am not certain what all those numbers are supposed to mean, however."

"Numbers," I repeated to myself, hearing a voice in my head.

Among those hidden parameters is a value called the violation index. Administrator quickly discovered that she could utilize this value to sniff out people who were skeptical of the Taboo Index she had set forth...

That had been from wise little Cardinal in the Great Library. This proved it: The Rebelling Index, as the box-people called it in the sacred tongue, was that very violation quotient she mentioned. All the dozens of "boxen" in this chamber were monitoring the values of every man, woman, and child in the world.

If they detected abnormal values, they would open a portal and peer into the location, identifying and reporting the violator. Then whoever received that report would order an Integrity Knight to bring that individual to justice. That was how Eugeo, Alice, and I were brought to the cathedral in the first place...

I was broken out of my stunned stupor by the sound of some kind of buzzer. Alice and I both tensed and raised our swords, but we hadn't been spotted. The boxen stopped their chanting and all looked upward.

Until now, I hadn't noticed that, on the walls just over their heads, faucet-like objects jutted upward. The box-people all opened their mouths, and a thick brown liquid abruptly flowed out of the spigots. They caught the liquid in their gaping mouths and swallowed it mechanically. Some of the liquid spilled out of their lips, staining necks and collarbones. That was likely the source of the stench.

Soon the buzzer sounded again, and that was the end of the liquid feeding. Their faces snapped forward again, and the chanting resumed: *System Call...System Call...*

This is no way to treat human beings.

In fact, even cattle and sheep shouldn't have been treated this way, I recognized with a surge of anger pulsing up from my gut. I clenched my teeth.

Alice grunted, "Are they...the senators who help the Axiom Church rule over the human realm...?"

I looked over to see that her one visible eye was shining with fury. I hadn't put that idea together, but it seemed accurate now. All of these dozens of people stuffed in boxes were the senators, the high administrative officers of the Axiom Church.

"And was it...the pontifex who created what I am seeing now?" she continued.

"I reckon it was," I said. "I bet she found people from all over the realm who were weak in combat skills but excellent in sacred arts, then stole their thoughts and emotions and turned them into this senatorial security system..."

System was right. These weren't people; they were devices. Their job was to maintain perfect peace—or stagnation—across the realm under the Axiom Church's rule. Even the Integrity Knights, with their most precious memories stolen, didn't suffer such an ignoble fate. It was atop centuries of this sacrifice that Administrator had reigned.

Alice slowly hung her head, until her dangling hair hid her expression.

"...This is unforgivable."

The Osmanthus Blade in her right hand rang softly, as though channeling its master's rage.

"No matter the crime, these are still human beings. But she did more than steal their memories—she removed the very intelligence and emotion that makes them human, stuffed them into these cages, and now feeds them worse than beasts…There can be no honor or justice here."

She raised her head to a noble tilt and strode willfully into the chamber. I rushed after her.

The senators' eyes did not move from their Stacia Windows, even with the shining presence of a beautiful lady knight in the darkness. She walked to her left and stood before one of the boxes. I watched the pale face of the senator over her shoulder.

Up close, there was no way to tell even a gender, much less an age. The endless period of captivity in this lightless prison had robbed all traces of humanity.

Alice lifted the Osmanthus Blade. I thought she was going to destroy the box at first, but instead she rested the tip right around the location of where the senator's heart would be. I gasped and hissed, "Alice!"

"Wouldn't it be a mercy…to end this life?"

I couldn't answer.

Even if we returned their memory fragments—assuming such things had even been saved—it seemed impossible that it would return them to their former selves. I had to assume that the senators' fluctlights had been broken beyond repair, twisted into something unrecognizable and wrong.

But even then, perhaps Cardinal or even Administrator herself could grant them some wish aside from death. It was this thought that made me reach out for her shoulder guard to stop her.

But just as I did, a strange sound from farther into the chamber caused us to freeze.

"Aaah…*Aaaaah!*"

It was a high-pitched, grating screech.

"Aaah, oh my, ohhh, Your Holiness, what a waste…Ohhhh, ahhh, you musn't, aaah, *ooooh!!*" howled the bizarre voice. Alice and I shared a suspicious look.

I didn't recognize it. It didn't sound young, but it didn't sound elderly, either. All I could tell from its voice was that it seemed to be in the throes of some kind of maniacal excitement.

Her anger temporarily forgotten, Alice lowered her sword and stared in the direction of the sound. The screeching voice was coming from another hallway in the wall, just like the one we came through but deeper inside the cylindrical room.

"..."

Alice pointed toward the hallway with her sword, motioning me on. I nodded, and we began to lurk toward it.

There were no pillars or furniture of any kind in the wide-open chamber, so crossing it was mildly terrifying, but none of the dozens of senators along the walls paid us any mind or seemed capable of recognizing our presence at all. Their entire world was the system window in front and the food spigot overhead, and that was it. I remembered feeling twinges of pity at the lives of the basement jailer and the girl controlling the elevated platform, but the word *pity* on its own was entirely inadequate to describe the plight of these creatures.

As for whoever was moaning and screeching at the top of their lungs right near this dehumanizing place, I couldn't begin to fathom the mindset. Whoever it was, I couldn't imagine them being an ally of any kind.

Alice felt so, too, and there was a different kind of anger now creeping over her pale face. She crossed the chamber on a straight line and peered around the side of the corridor, while I stole a look over her shoulder.

At the end of the similarly cramped hallway was another large room, albeit much smaller than the circular chamber. The light inside was soft but bright enough to make out its contents.

And they were absolutely bizarre.

Every last fixture of the room shone in garish gold, from cabinets and beds to little round chairs and storage boxes, all reflecting the light in equal measure. Even from this distance, I could feel it penetrating my eyeballs to the back of my head.

A plethora of toys in every size was scattered all over—in some cases spilling out of—this furniture. Most were stuffed animals in bold primary colors. There were dolls with button eyes and yarn hair, familiar animals like pets and livestock, even some hideous monsters I couldn't begin to identify, heaped into piles all over the floor and beds. There were building blocks, a wooden horse, instruments—like the entire stock from the District Five toy maker had been dumped here.

And sitting half-buried in them, facing away from us, was the voice's owner.

"Hoooooo!! *Hooooooo!!*" it screamed, over and over. This figure, too, had a bizarre appearance.

It was round, almost a perfect sphere of a torso, with a round head on top, like a snowman. But rather than being white, the body was clad in a clown's outfit, with the right half bright red, and the left blue. The short-armed sleeves had red-and-blue stripes, as well. It was making my eyes hurt.

The round head was completely white, and from the rear it looked no different from the senators', except that the skin was oily and shiny. Resting atop the head was a golden cap the same shade as all the furniture.

I leaned over Alice's ear and whispered, "Is that the prime senator...?"

"Yes, it's Chudelkin," she whispered back, but with an audible loathing. I stared at the clown's back again.

The prime senator was a kind of counterpart to Bercouli the commander of the knights, the greatest caster of sacred arts in the Axiom Church and one of its chief officers. And yet, he seemed totally defenseless. Whatever was in his hands, it had his entire attention.

From what I could make out beyond his very round back, Chudelkin was gazing into a large crystal ball. With each flash of color inside, he flopped and kicked his little legs and shrieked, "Haaa! Hohhh!"

I'd been expecting a tense and uncertain lead-up to a spectacular battle, like with Deusolbert and Fanatio, so I had no idea how to react to this. But while I wasn't sure how to proceed, Alice had no such hesitation. She raced toward him, not even bothering to sneak.

But her feet hit the ground only five times. She easily brushed me off and raced like a golden gust into the toy room, and by the time Chudelkin's fat head started to turn, she already had the frilly collar of his clown outfit clutched in her fist.

"Hooooo?!" the round object howled. Alice yanked him out of the sea of plushies and held him high. At last, I caught up to her and, glancing around the entire room, looked for any sign of Eugeo—but wherever Chudelkin had brought my partner after the Great Bath, it wasn't here. Disappointed, I turned back to the middle, where the crystal ball that had so enraptured the strange little man caught my eye.

A somewhat three-dimensional image wreathed in swirling light was projected in the center of the large glass ball, which was about a foot and a half across. It displayed a girl sprawled on her side atop lustrous bedsheets. Her face was hidden behind long silver hair, but it was clear from a glance that she wasn't wearing a stitch of clothing.

Both disappointed and fulfilled that this was what Chudelkin had been exclaiming over, I then noticed that there seemed to be someone else with the girl. I tried to lean in for a closer look, but the spell vanished, the images inside the ball abruptly flashing into whiteness.

Alice had no interest in the crystal ball to begin with. With her free hand, she thrust the tip of her sword toward the dangling man and threatened, "If you try to start chanting an art, I'll cut your tongue out from the root."

The little man clamped his mouth shut before any complaints could arise. Given that all sacred arts in the Underworld had to begin with the System Call prefix, the caster was essentially at our mercy now. Still, I paid close attention to his stumpy arms for any movement and glanced up quickly to get a view of Prime Senator Chudelkin.

I couldn't imagine a more enigmatic human face. His bright-red lips dominated the lower half of his round face, with a large bulb of a nose, and eyes and brows as curved as an iconic smiley face.

Those beady eyes were bulging now, though, the small, dark pupils jittering as they stared right at Alice. Eventually he relaxed his heavy lips from their trumpeter's sour pucker and screeched in tones of rusted metal, "You...Number Thirty...What are you doing here? You fell out of the tower with the other rebel and plummeted to your death!"

"Don't call me by a number! My name is Alice—and I am not Thirty any longer," she snapped, her voice freezing air. Chudelkin's greasy face twitched, and for the first time, he looked at me. His crescent-shaped eyes bulged out to half-moons, and he gurgled a series of gasps.

"You...Why—what is this?! Number Thir...Alice, why do you not attack this boy?! He is a rebel against the Church...an agent of the Dark Territory, as I warned you!!"

"He is indeed a rebel. But he is no soldier of the dark lands. He is just like me."

"Wha...? Wha...?"

Chudelkin's stumpy arms and legs flopped around in midair like the toys that filled the room. "You—you would *dare* to rebel against us, you little piece of *shit*!!"

His round white head instantly turned beet red, and his scream reached an even higher register than before, the sword pointed at his throat entirely forgotten.

"You Integrity Knights are nothing but mindless puppets!! You don't move until I *command* you to move!! And now you have the *gall* to rebel against our glorious leader, my lady Administrator herself?!"

Alice snapped her head to the side to avoid the spittle flying from Chudelkin's apoplectic lips, but she did not otherwise react to his insults. "It was the Axiom Church that turned us into puppets," she stated coldly. "The Synthesis Ritual blocked our memories, instilled loyalty into us by force, and made us believe the lie that we were knights summoned to earth from Heaven."

"Wha…?" Chudelkin's face went from red back to white, his large mouth flapping helplessly. "Why…? How did you…?"

"Blocked or not, there are a few memories I still retain. When we stepped into the senate room, I caught a glimpse of an image…A terrified girl tied up in the center of that chamber, subjected to three days and nights of the senators' multilayered spells to crack open the walls of her mind. That was the truth of the Synthesis Ritual…and the stone floor of that chamber is most certainly stained with the tears of lamentation and despair of that girl I once was."

Alice's voice was controlled, but it cut like a steel blade. Chudelkin's face bounced back and forth between red and white at a dizzying speed. Ultimately, the only person in the senate with his own will regained his swagger and leered at us.

"Oh yes…that is correct. I can recall the scene quite clearly, in fact. You were so young and innocent and sweet, and you pleaded with tears in your eyes so many times…'Please, don't let me forget…Don't let me forget the people I care about!' Hoh-hoh-hoh-hoh!"

When he put on a hideous falsetto to mimic a little girl's speech, Alice's eye grew bright with flame. This did not threaten Chudelkin into stopping his mockery.

"Oh-ho! Oh-ho! Yes, I remember indeed! Even now, I could spend an entire night basking in the delicious memory! They dragged you out of that rural hellhole you called a home, and I put you to work as an apprentice sister for two years. You were the kind of tomboy who would slip through the curfew regulations and go see the Centoria solstice festival, but you really *truly* believed that if you studied hard, we'd let you go home again. Of course, that wasn't true in the least! Just when you raised that sacred arts authority level to a good solid amount, *boom!* Forced synthesis! Oh, you should have seen the look on your face when you learned you'd never go home again…I wish I could have turned you into stone and kept you around as a decoration in my chamber forever! Hoh-hoh-hoh!!"

Even I couldn't stop my sword arm from trembling. I heard Alice grinding her teeth over Chudelkin's jabs, but she kept herself under control and said, "You mentioned something odd just now: forced synthesis. That makes it sound like there's a voluntary version of the Synthesis Ritual."

The prime senator's eyes narrowed into slits. "Hoh-hoh, very shrewd of you. Yes, that's correct. Six years ago, you steadfastly refused to recite any of the secret commands that are necessary for a typical Synthesis Ritual. You actually had the nerve to tell me your calling was still back in your home village and that you didn't need to obey my orders!"

That sounds just like what young Alice would say, I thought, despite having not known her back then. The memory of this experience caused the prime senator's lips to curl into a nasty sneer.

"What a disgusting little shit you were. I wished so badly to have my lady awaken early, but the rule is that she's not to rise until all the preparations for the ritual are completely done. So I had no choice but to temporarily pause the automated senators and have them pry open the door to your most *precious* secrets through magical force. I suppose I shouldn't complain about getting such a juicy show, however! Hee-hoh, hoh-hohhh!"

His gale of laughter stopped the instant she moved the tip of the Osmanthus Blade an inch closer. But the ugly smirk on his lips and in his eyes remained.

Chudelkin had boasted several crucial bits of information. I wanted to pry out some more intel, assuming Alice could maintain her composure, but something about it felt wrong. Would this clown really reveal core secrets of the Church without even being prompted? He wouldn't taunt her this way if he was afraid for his life, and he didn't seem to be waiting for a chance to take her by surprise, either.

While my mind raced on, Chudelkin resumed his story. "When

the first stage of the forced synthesis ended and you blacked out, it was none other than I who took you to Her Holiness. Regrettably, I was not allowed to witness what happened next, but when the ritual was done and you awoke as an Integrity Knight, you had total belief that you were a disciple of God, dispatched from Heaven. Just like all the other knights. Boy, when I hear you folks drone on and on about the celestial realm, I have to hold my sides in to keep them from splitting! Ohhh…"

He babbled and chattered away, dangling in the air, and I gradually noticed that his eyes were jittering slightly, as though he were waiting for something. Was he carrying on like this in order to keep us here in the room with him…?

I was about to warn Alice, but she spoke first. The golden room rang with her voice, even icier now than in the Great Bath: "Prime Senator Chudelkin, you may be just another victim like the Integrity Knights, a sad little clown whose life was a plaything for Administrator like everyone else. But regardless of that, you have enjoyed your circumstances immensely. Surely you have been satisfied with your life. I am done listening to you."

The Osmanthus Blade's tip pressed against the center of the bulging clown costume, right above his heart. The shining material dipped inward with one final show of resistance.

If Chudelkin's goal was to buy time, he would bring up some new piece of information now, I assumed—perhaps Eugeo's location.

But one second was all it took to prove me wrong.

As the prime senator froze, his mouth half-open, the golden sword plunged deeper and deeper. His narrow eyes shot wide open, and the red-and-blue outfit bulged out even farther, testing its limits. Alice turned her face away, anticipating a spray of blood.

There was a tremendous *bang!* and Chudelkin's body popped like a balloon. A massive gush of blood landed on Alice's armor and did…nothing.

"What…?"

"Huh?!"

Alice and I were stunned. It was not liquid that burst forth, but smoke that had somehow been colored deep red. It spread farther and farther, filling the room.

There had been a special kind of monster in Aincrad that did this. It puffed out the skin of its body, and if struck with any kind of non-blunt damage, it would burst and emit a huge blast of smoke, allowing its true body to escape.

With that old instinct in mind, I swung my sword at a narrow shadow that quickly passed the corner of my vision. I felt it strike something, but the only object I could see through the smoke was a familiar golden hat rolling at my feet.

I made to chase after him, but the moment the nasty-colored smoke entered my nostrils, I felt a needling pain in my throat and doubled over coughing.

"Chudelkin!" Alice hissed, hand over her mouth, and leaped for the shadow. Chudelkin ran toward the back of the chamber, not toward the hallway to the senate room. I followed after them in a crouch, believing there wasn't actually an exit back there.

Instead, the first thing I saw when I got through the choking smoke was a golden chest of drawers pushed to the side to reveal a hidden passage. A comically thin figure with that same fat round head was nimbly racing down it.

"Hee-hoh!! Heeee-hee-hee-hee-hee-hoh!!" he cackled, loud enough that I could hear it through my coughing. "Sacred arts isn't all I'm good at, you pathetic losers! Sucks to be you! Wanna play tag? Because I can play the host, and I'm very thorough! Hoh-hohhhhhh!!"

The pattering of his shoes soon drowned out his maniacal, broken-toy laughter.

4

Alice and I were slowed down for less than five seconds.

We shared a glance, then I took the lead down the narrow hallway. Thankfully, the red smoke I inhaled wasn't toxic—if it had been, something would've happened to Chudelkin, given that his clothes were filled with the stuff—and the coughing indeed soon wore off.

The hidden passage was built for Chudelkin's size, and I had to duck down to avoid hitting my head on the ceiling. The occasional scraping noise I heard from behind had to be Alice's shoulder guards hitting the walls. The sheath of the Blue Rose Sword on my right waist was also banging against the wall as I shuffled along uncomfortably.

Eventually there was an ascending staircase ahead, so I stopped and made sure there wasn't an ambush before charging upward. Chudelkin's footsteps were long gone, darkness and cold air the only things coming down the passage ahead.

The staircase was much longer than I had anticipated and seemed to cover a good three floors' worth of height. I'd estimated that the chamber filled with what Chudelkin called the *automated senators* covered the space from the ninety-sixth to ninety-eighth floors, so this path was probably leading us up to the ninety-ninth.

The battle with the Axiom Church that had begun in the

basement—two years before, when Eugeo and I left Rulid—would be over in two floors. My partner wasn't at my side, but if Bercouli's words were accurate, I would see him again in Administrator's bedchamber. Then I'd give him the Blue Rose Sword, and the three of us would defeat Chudelkin, then the pontifex herself. And then...

I shook my head, focusing on a faint light up above. I could think about what to do afterward when we got there. This was the final battle: Concentration was everything, and the present was more important than the future and the past.

From up ahead, I heard the distant screech of the prime senator.

"System Caaaaall! Generaaaate..."

That would be an element-based sacred art. My hackles rose, but there was no stopping now. The light ahead grew closer and closer.

"The stairs are ending up ahead!" I warned Alice.

"Watch out for a surprise arts attack!" she replied.

"Got it!"

I held my black sword out front as I ran. Given the measure of control a caster had over the possession of a generated element, magic in this world was well suited to ambush attacks. You could form a flame element, keep it on standby, then discharge it when the enemy came into sight, almost like a firearm.

On the other hand, the power of the magic was dependent upon the number of elements being expended. If it was just one little orb, the attack power would be the same, whether cast by a student in their first year at school or a master with a lifetime of experience. Discipline allowed one to increase the number of elements at once, but each one required a finger to maintain it, so the upper limit of simultaneous elements was ten. My black sword had the capability to absorb energy, so I could defend against even a tenfold heat or frost element attack.

If Chudelkin was going to attempt a surprise attack, it would be safer to plunge through the exit of the stairway, rather than lean out carefully. I sped up through the last leg and leaped high in the air on the final step.

But there was no storm of fireballs or deluge of icicles. I did a full three-sixty turn in midair to survey the room, but I did not see Chudelkin or anyone else. I landed on the marble floor on one knee and listened carefully. The only sound was Alice running toward me.

She appeared through the exit of the staircase as I got to my feet, then she took her own turn examining the place. "I thought I heard him chanting, but there's no one here…Perhaps Chudelkin gave up on laying a trap and fled to the hundredth floor above…," she murmured, glancing up at the ceiling.

"But that's Administrator's room, right?" I asked. "Is the prime senator allowed to just burst in there?"

"I doubt it…Where are the stairs up anyway?"

Once again, I looked around the round room that composed the ninety-ninth floor. It was quite large, probably a hundred feet across. The floor, ceiling, and curved walls were the same familiar white marble, but there was nothing in the way of decoration or ornamentation. At most, there was a series of large lamps fixed to the walls, but only four were lit, leaving the interior dim. Everything in the room was pure white, so it would probably be blinding in here if all the lamps were on at once.

The staircase we'd taken opened directly into the floor near the wall. There was a marble hatch above, and I was certain that if lowered, it would fit seamlessly into the floor.

Perhaps there was a similar hidden drop-down door in the ceiling somewhere. I looked around for a pull cord or handle, but saw nothing. Perhaps a good sword skill might punch a hole in the ceiling…

"This room," Alice suddenly murmured. I turned and saw that the knight's left eye was open wider than usual.

"What about it?"

"I've…been in here before. This is where I woke up…on the day I became an apprentice Integrity Knight…"

"W-wait…are you sure about that?!"

"Yes…All the lamps were on at the time…and the room was

extremely bright and shining…The pontifex herself stood in the center, and she commanded, *Wake up, child of God…*"

Alice realized that a note of reverence had crept into her voice, and she scowled. "The pontifex removed all my memories up to that point, gave me a false past and a knight's duty, then left me with Uncle…with Commander Bercouli. Then a part of the floor, similar to the elevating disc in the middle part of the cathedral, took Uncle and me down to the ninety-fifth floor. I have never been back here since."

"The floor…sank?" I repeated, stomping on the marble with my boots. The only sensation I felt was thick, unmoving stone. It would be hard to find a hidden elevator in a room this size, and we didn't need to go *down*.

"Do you remember how Administrator went back to her chamber then, Alice?" I asked.

She lifted a finger to her lips and thought. "I think…that the moment the disc sank into the floor…she looked up…and another small disc descended from above…"

"That's it!" I shouted, staring greedily at the white ceiling. It wasn't a pull-down hatch but an elevator hidden above us. Even still, I couldn't spot anything like a switch. There wasn't an operator like on the elevator between the fiftieth and eightieth floors, so there had to be some mechanism to work it automatically. But what was it…?

"Oh…perhaps it was what the prime senator was chanting…," I wondered aloud. Alice latched onto it.

"So it wasn't an ambush but an art to make the disc move…? Kirito, what did you hear Chudelkin say after 'Generate'? Do you remember?"

I really, really didn't want to tell her *I wasn't listening*, so I frantically replayed the moment from a few minutes before in my head. His needle-pitched voice had cried, *Generate*, and then…

"L…Lu…something…," I said, struggling to remember. Alice's glare was even colder than usual.

"That should be enough. The only element that starts with *lu* would be a light element."

My face lit up, and I nodded to show that I did understand after all, but Alice was already turning and putting away her sword. She thrust her open hands toward the ceiling.

"System Call! Generate Luminous Element!"

To my amazement, she created a full ten light elements, the theoretical maximum. She then sprayed the floating white orbs outward without further modification. They landed at various points on the ceiling and burst without a sound. One flashed brighter than before—and then a circle of light a few feet across appeared where it had landed. It wasn't in the center of the room, but close to the wall.

Alice lowered her arms, and I walked up to her side, watching cautiously. The circle of light faded quickly but did not disappear, and before long, the ceiling within its perimeter slid smoothly down toward us.

The stone platform was at least eighteen inches thick and looked tremendously heavy, yet it floated as if it were nothing. The light element had merely been a switch, and something else was powering the movement, but I couldn't begin to guess what it was. It was on the level of some of the "miracles" I saw Cardinal perform in the Great Library—in fact, that must be exactly what it was. The source of this elevator's movement was doubtless some tiny piece of Administrator's boundless power.

The elevator landed on the floor with the slightest of vibrations. The top was not bare marble but was covered in bright-red carpet that glowed faintly in the light coming down from the circular hole in the ceiling.

The way to the top floor of Central Cathedral was open.

When Alice and I rode that elevating disc to the hundredth floor, the last and biggest battle of all would begin.

The original plan was that I'd use my secret-weapon dagger on Administrator while she slept and let Cardinal handle the rest. But with Chudelkin hiding from us on the floor above, she would likely be awake already—and more importantly, I'd already used my dagger to save Fanatio, the vice commander of the Integrity Knights.

Fortunately—if you could call it that—Alice the knight had agreed to return to being the original Alice already. That meant Eugeo didn't need to use his dagger on her. When we got up there, I'd have to rescue him from his frozen state, I suspected, and find a way to use his dagger before Administrator started taking me seriously. I couldn't imagine another way for us to win.

Alice was reaching a final moment of determination as well. We stared at each other and nodded in unison.

"...Let's go."

"Here goes nothing."

And thus the elite disciple Kirito and Integrity Knight Alice Synthesis Thirty started walking toward the elevating disc that awaited just ahead.

One, two, three steps—and the pale light coming from the hole in the ceiling, probably moonlight, abruptly shaded over.

I stopped and stared into the hole, where I caught sight of a number of bright glimmers of light.

It was, in fact, moonlight—reflecting off a beautifully designed suit of armor. Whoever it was leaped down through the hole, a good twenty feet above, long cape trailing behind.

It was too tall to be Chudelkin. Then I wondered whether Administrator was coming down to this floor, but the figure's stature was male. I couldn't make out a face against the light.

"Are there more Integrity Knights left?" I muttered.

"That armor belongs to...No, wait...," Alice whispered, right as the descending knight landed atop the disc. He bent his knees to absorb the impact and slowly straightened back up.

The armor was silver tinged with blue. The metal plate looked almost a bit translucent, collecting the moonlight and bouncing it back beautifully. The cape was deep blue, and I did not see a sword on his waist. His downturned face was hidden behind a large gorget covering his neck, but the wavy hair was...a soft flaxen color.

Instantly, a shock like a bolt of lightning shot through me.

That color. I'd lived for two years in the Underworld with that hair color right nearby.

It can't be. But. How...

I was caught flat-footed, locked in extreme confusion. At last, the knight raised his head, and his green eyes looked at me through heavy lids. There was no longer any room for doubt. The young man in the Integrity Knight armor was...

".........Eugeo........."

The name left my mouth as barely more than a moan.

I would never mistake him for anyone else. He was my partner and my best friend; we'd been inseparable since our meeting in the forest two years ago. The only thing that kept me going for so long in this alternate world was Eugeo's presence at my side. I would never, ever see his features in someone else's face by accident.

But this expression in Eugeo's eyes and mouth as he stared at me was one I did not recognize. In fact, it was not an expression at all—the word implied that something was actively being expressed. This youth was all inanimate ice, even colder than when we'd first met Alice at the practice hall of Swordcraft Academy.

"Eugeo," I repeated, my voice normal this time. The cold glare did not falter or break in the least. But he wasn't ignoring me. He was measuring me, testing me...to see whether I was worthy of the bite of his weapon.

"...No...it's too soon," Alice mumbled.

Desperate for anything to cling to, I asked, "Soon...? Too soon for what...?"

"For the completion of the ritual," the golden knight said, glancing at me only briefly before she announced, "Your partner... Eugeo has *already been synthesized.*"

The Synthesis Ritual. Direct manipulation of the fluctlight, a process only Administrator was capable of. Stealing memories, inserting loyalty...raising him into an Integrity Knight.

"...No...no way...You said it took three days and nights," I protested, shaking my head like a stubborn child.

"The prime senator said that was because I refused to recite the necessary sacred arts commands. If I had simply repeated them, that three-day process would not have been necessary...But even still, this is too soon. Barely hours have passed since Eugeo fought Uncle..."

"That's right...This isn't possible. Eugeo couldn't...just...It has to be some kind of illusion art or something..."

I took an uncertain step forward, not even fully comprehending what I was saying anymore. I was jolted to attention by Alice reaching out to grab my right arm. "Get a grip!" she hissed. "If you can't stay calm, we'll lose any chance we might have to save him!"

"S...save...?"

"That's right! You yourself said it: There is a way to restore the knight's original memories! So there must be a way to return Eugeo to normal! We *must* overcome this challenge in order to take advantage of that!!" she spat out, her palm burning with pure willpower against my wrist and pouring life back into my numb flesh. I'd nearly been about to drop my sword; I gripped it harder than ever.

Alice was right. Eugeo's memory and persona weren't lost forever. They just couldn't come to the surface, due to the manipulation of a single part of his fluctlight.

All I had to do was take back the Memory Fragment that Administrator stole from him and have Cardinal reintegrate it, and then Eugeo would return to the gentle, mild-mannered swordsman I knew. The first step to achieving that would be dialogue and information gathering. Whatever personality was running Eugeo, I had to convince it to let us pass...or perhaps even help us. I'd been completely helpless against Alice, and somehow I had won her over with words—there must be a way to repeat that success.

"...Let me handle this," I whispered to Alice, who was still clutching my wrist. Hesitantly, she acquiesced and let go.

"All right. But don't take him lightly. That knight is no longer the Eugeo you knew."

"Right," I said. Alice took a step back.

To be honest, no matter how powerful Eugeo was as an Integrity Knight, as long as Alice used her Perfect Weapon Control—transforming the Osmanthus Blade into a storm of petals that tore the enemy to shreds—we could easily neutralize his strength. Such was the power of Alice's ability. But that was truly the last resort, after all other options had been exhausted. I wanted to avoid harming him if at all possible, and it seemed the height of cruelty to make two childhood friends fight when their memories of each other were stolen.

I stepped forward and took the full brunt of Eugeo's cold stare.

"Eugeo," I said for the third time, completely firm, "do you remember me? I'm Kirito...your partner. Remember how we've been together for the entire past two years?"

The young man in blue-and-silver armor said nothing for several moments, until...

"I'm sorry, I don't know you."

That was the first thing Eugeo the Integrity Knight said to me. His soft voice was as I remembered, but it had the same icy quality as his eyes. Clearly he had no access to his pre-synthesis memories, but surely the quick process meant there wasn't time to insert the usual false memories about being summoned from Heaven, either. There must have been a huge blank space in Eugeo's self-conception at the moment. If I could just take advantage of that...

"But thank you," he continued, to my surprise.

Suddenly full of hope at that non-hostile response, I asked, "For what?"

"For bringing me my sword," he said.

"Uh..."

I looked down to my right side. There was the Blue Rose Sword, a Divine Object wrapped in its white leather sheath. I looked up and asked, "What are you...going to do with it?"

Eugeo's green eyes blinked, and he said, quite simply, "I'm going to fight you. That's what she wants."

"…"

Then it was true—he had come down into this room to defeat Alice and me. Because it was what *she* wanted.

Sensing that my hopes were growing further and further away, I still clung on. "Eugeo, are you just going to follow orders…to fight without knowing who you are or even the meaning of that fight? We are not your enemies. You came all this way to fight Administrator and take back your precious—"

"It doesn't matter what the meaning is," he said, and for the briefest of moments, he wore the first true expression I had seen. "She is going to give me what I want. And that is all I need."

"What you want…? Is it something more precious than Alice?"

The moment he heard that name, supposedly the most important thing in his world, I thought I sensed a flicker of emotion in his pale features. But again, he covered it up with that icy visage.

"I don't know. I don't want to know. About you…or anyone. I'm just sick…of…already…," he mumbled, the words too faint for me to make out. He stepped off the disc and held out his hand. "I have nothing more to say to you. Let's fight…That's why you're here, isn't it?"

"…Not to fight with you, Eugeo. I can't give back this sword," I warned him in hushed tones, switching my black sword over to my left hand and pulling out the Blue Rose Sword with my right. With my eyes trained on Eugeo, I reached toward Alice behind me and—

"I don't need it transferred by hand."

The white sheath was ripped from my hand. But it wasn't Alice. The sword shot through the air, as though pulled by invisible strings, and landed right in Eugeo's grasp, over thirty feet away.

Sacred arts?! Did I miss him chanting…?!

Then I heard a voice behind me spout, "Incarnate Arms…!"

"What's that?" I asked, face still forward.

"It's an ancient art taught to the Integrity Knights," she explained quickly. "It is neither sacred art nor Perfect Weapon

Control. It simply moves objects with the force of will alone. I've heard that only a few knights aside from Uncle can use it."

"You mean you can't?"

"I...I trained in it, but I can't even move a pebble, much less a Divine Object. There's no way a brand-new knight could master it so quickly..."

All the while, Eugeo was examining the Blue Rose Sword, and he hung the sheath on his left side. He grabbed the hilt and promptly drew it. The faintly translucent blade gave off a white mist of frosty air.

I had no choice but to put my normal sword back in the proper hand and hold it up. Eugeo and I had faced off many times over the past two years. But that was always with wooden practice swords; we had never once used the black sword and Blue Rose Sword against each other.

And yet, the only feeling that filled my chest was the realization that the time had finally arrived. I'd sensed this moment might come, on the very day we left Rulid. But that vision was only to the point that our blades clashed. The outcome of the fight was still unwritten. And no one else—not even Administrator—could decide that for us.

"Eugeo," I said, considering this to be our final conversation, "you might not remember this, but I was the one who taught you to use the sword. And I can't afford to lose to my own pupil."

He didn't say anything back. He merely lifted the Blue Rose Sword and assumed the pose to initiate a sword skill: the one-handed charge attack, Sonic Leap.

Slightly pleased that he still remembered the Aincrad moves I'd taught him, even after he'd forgotten his own name, I made the same stance.

Two swords glowed the same shade of light green.

One second later, Eugeo and I launched off the marble floor in unison.

(To be continued)

AFTERWORD

Hello, this is Reki Kawahara. Thank you for reading *Sword Art Online 13: Alicization Dividing.*

This is now the fifth volume of the Alicization arc, and with the introduction of the big bad, I can finally heave a sigh of relief... which I probably shouldn't be wasting my time with. Like the previous volume, there's a lot of going up and down here. I chose different kanji for *climbing* a wall and *climbing* stairs, which made my own proofing efforts very difficult to keep track of—not to mention the poor proofreaders!

Sorry, got off track there. We've been having difficulty just getting to the big boss fight, and this volume is finally where we get a good up-close look at Alice Synthesis Thirty, the third protagonist and the inspiration for the series subtitle. How she faces the systems that bind her and how she attempts to create her own fate are major themes of this story, so I hope that you can get behind her the same way that you do for Kirito and Eugeo.

Speaking of Eugeo, he got a sudden class upgrade at the very last moment, didn't he? Can Kirito defeat him as a mere swordsman, or will he need to look into a class change of his own? My usual apologies for ending us right at that cliffhanger! We will finally be fighting Administrator in Volume 14—the wait is nearly over!

...And this is where I must sadly admit that the next *SAO* book will be *Progressive*, Volume 2. If you've grown tired of Kirito and Asuna being split up between the Underworld and real life, you'll be able to read about them tackling the third floor of Aincrad in that one. Please check it out.

And now, a brief advertisement. As of this writing (2013), there will be an end-of-year TV special for the *SAO* anime. It's going to be a recap of the Aincrad and Fairy Dance arcs from the 2012 TV series, but there will be some new animation included. It's the first time in a year that Kirito has graced the screen in motion, so be sure to tune in.

Lastly, to my illustrator abec, who had to deal with my usual lateness, my editors Mr. Miki and Mr. Tsuchiya, and everyone who's read this far, thank you so much. See you in the next book!

Reki Kawahara—June 2013